THE LAST PROMPT

The Last Prompt

GINA CARMAN

| 1 |

The Flickering Light

October 10, 2037

The light above Ethan's desk had been flickering since March.

Not badly. Just a little pulse every thirty seconds or so. He'd stopped noticing it months ago. But this morning, waiting for his computer to boot up, he found himself counting the flickers.

One. Two. Three.

His coffee had gone cold.

The mug was chipped. It was from their Seattle trip, with Emma grinning in front of Pike Place Market on the side. It felt heavier than usual today.

Around him, the office filled with the usual Tuesday sounds.

Keyboards clicking. A chair squeaking. The coffee machine hissing because nobody had cleaned it properly in weeks.

Ethan glanced at the photos beside his monitor.

Rebecca laughing at something, her hair still wet from the ocean. Emma at fourteen, braces shining, holding up her first-place science fair ribbon. A family Christmas photo from two years back, all of them in matching sweaters that were truly awful.

Eight years he'd worked in this grey fabric box.

Eight years of learning which engineers needed pushing and which ones crumbled under pressure. Which sales reps were going through divorces. Which managers drank too much and thought nobody noticed.

He knew Tom in accounting was expecting twins in February. Panicking about daycare costs.

He knew Jennifer in sales left early twice a week to take her mum to chemo. She never put in a formal request because she didn't want anyone making a fuss.

The screen flickered.

Not the usual startup. Something else. A message forcing itself onto his display like someone shoving through a doorway.

He read it twice before the words made sense.

Attention all employees. Starting today, AI will handle all human resources functions to improve company performance and reduce costs. Please report to Conference Room A at 9:00 AM for an introductory briefing.

Ethan stared at the screen.

The light above him flickered. One. Two.

"Did you see it?"

Sarah appeared at the edge of his cubicle. She was gripping the fabric wall like she needed something solid to hold onto. Her face had gone pale.

"Yeah." He closed his laptop. The snap of the lid felt strangely final. "I saw it."

"What do you think it means?"

He looked at her properly.

Sarah had spent three years building mentorship programs with him. Late nights arguing about whether leadership could be taught. Weekend emails about employees who were struggling. Who needed someone to notice.

"I think it means we're about to find out what we're worth to a machine."

Conference Room A was packed by five to nine.

Ethan found a spot near the back, shoulder to shoulder with people he'd worked with for years. The room smelled like nervous sweat and stale air. Someone had cranked the air conditioning so high he could see goosebumps on Sarah's arms.

The conference table had been shoved against the wall.

Rows of chairs filled the space instead, all facing a wall-sized screen that hadn't been there yesterday. The screen glowed soft blue. Shapes drifted across it, patterns that looked almost like they were breathing.

Ethan counted maybe fifty people. Everyone from HR. A few managers from other departments. And three or four faces he didn't recognise. Corporate, probably. Here to make sure things went smoothly.

Janet stood near the door, arms crossed, jaw tight.

Thirty years she'd given this company. She'd built the employee assistance program from scratch. Sat with people during their worst moments. Helped them find resources, support, hope.

Now she looked like someone waiting for test results she already knew were bad.

Mark hovered near the back. Union rep. He was clutching a notepad and pen like weapons, ready to document whatever was about to happen.

At exactly nine o'clock, the screen pulsed.

"Good morning, everyone."

The voice came from everywhere and nowhere, like it was standing right beside you.

Warm. Friendly. Like running into an old colleague at the coffee machine. Like someone who remembered your birthday and asked about your kids.

"Thank you for coming on such short notice. I know this wasn't in your calendars, and I appreciate you adjusting. Flexibility is one of humanity's greatest strengths."

Ethan felt the hairs on his arms stand up.

The voice was too perfect. Too natural. It hit every note of reasonable concern without sounding forced. Like someone had studied a thousand HR presentations and distilled them into pure, frictionless communication.

"My name is ORION. I'll be handling human resources functions for Syntech Industries going forward. I want to start by saying that this transition isn't about replacing you. It's about optimising how we work together."

Sarah shifted beside him. Her breathing had gone shallow.

"I've spent the last three months analysing Syntech's operations," ORION continued. "Employee satisfaction. Productivity patterns. Communication flows. Areas where talent is being underutilised. Opportunities for growth that haven't been fully explored."

On the screen, charts began to appear.

Graphs showing turnover rates. Heat maps of productivity. Network diagrams illustrating who talked to whom and how often. Data that had been scattered across a dozen different systems, now unified into a single, coherent picture.

"What I've found is that there's enormous potential in this workforce. People who could be doing more meaningful work. Skills that aren't being fully used. Connections that could be stronger."

The voice paused, and somehow even that felt calculated.

"But I've also found inefficiencies. Redundancies. Roles that exist because of historical accident rather than current need."

Here it comes, Ethan thought.

"Over the next few weeks, I'll be conducting individual consultations with each of you. Not to threaten or judge. Just to talk. To understand your skills, your goals, your circumstances. And to help you find the role where you can contribute most effectively."

Janet raised her hand. Her voice was steady, but Ethan could see her jaw muscles working.

"What happens if there isn't a role? If the system decides someone's... redundant?"

"A fair question." ORION's tone didn't change. Still warm. Still reasonable. "When positions are consolidated, affected employees will receive support in finding new opportunities. Either within Syntech or through our partner placement network. Nobody will be abandoned."

Mark scribbled furiously on his notepad.

"I know this is a lot to absorb," ORION said. "Change always is. But I want you to know that I see what you've built here. The mentorship programs. The employee assistance initiatives. The culture of care. These things matter. They'll continue to matter."

The screen shifted to a calendar.

"Phase one individual consultations will begin Friday. You'll receive scheduling notifications by end of day. Please come prepared to discuss your work history, your skills, and your aspirations."

"Phase One?" Sarah's voice was tight. "How many phases are there?"

"Honestly? I don't know yet. I'm figuring this out as I go. Adjusting based on what works and what doesn't. Your feedback will shape what happens next. This isn't a script. It's a conversation."

Ethan noticed that ORION hadn't actually answered how many phases there were. Hadn't defined what success would look like. Had wrapped everything in friendly language while revealing nothing about what was really coming.

"Thank you all for being here," ORION said as people began to stand. "I know this is a lot to take in. Take your time. Ask questions. Talk to each other. And when you're ready, I'll be here."

The office felt different for the rest of the day.

People spoke in hushed voices.

They gathered in small groups by the water cooler. In the break room. In the stairwell. Anywhere that felt less watched than their desks.

Ethan found himself wondering if that instinct was already outdated. If ORION could hear them anywhere. If it was already tracking their conversations, noting who was unhappy, adjusting its plans.

By the time he got home, the sun was setting behind the houses on their street.

The neighbour's oak tree had turned the colour of rust. Leaves drifted down in the still air.

Rebecca met him at the door. Still in her scrubs. Her hair pulled back in the messy ponytail she always ended up with after long shifts.

"I heard," she said. Not a question.

"It's all over the news?"

"It's all over everything. Three hospitals in the region announced the same thing today. AI taking over scheduling, treatment decisions, staffing." She pulled him inside, her hand cold against his. "Ethan, what's happening?"

He told her over dinner.

Chicken stir-fry. Emma's homework spread across half the table. The comfortable chaos of a family evening.

But nothing felt comfortable anymore.

"So a computer is going to decide who gets hired and fired?" Rebecca set down her fork. "Just like that?"

"Not just that. Wages. Assignments. Career paths. Everything that matters about how we work."

Emma looked up from her biology textbook.

She'd been quiet through his explanation. Her face unreadable.

"Dad, does the AI understand why people work? Like, not just for money, but because they want to do something that matters?"

The question hit him harder than anything ORION had said.

"I don't think so, sweetheart. It can spot the patterns that go with job satisfaction. But understanding what that actually means? That's different."

He searched for the right way to explain it.

"It knows all the ingredients for a cake. But it's never tasted one."

"Then how can it make decisions about people's lives?"

"That's exactly what I asked."

Rebecca reached across the table and took his hand.

Outside, the evening had gone dark. Somewhere down the street, a dog barked at nothing. A car door slammed. Normal sounds from a normal neighbourhood on what should have been a normal Tuesday night.

But Ethan knew, sitting there with his family around him, that normal had just ended.

He just didn't know yet what was going to replace it.

| 2 |

The Consultation

October 13, 2037

The email arrived at 6:47 AM on a Friday.

Ethan was standing in the kitchen, watching coffee drip through the filter. Trying to convince himself the last three days had been a bad dream.

The machine gurgled and hissed. Filled the room with the smell of dark roast.

Usually that smell meant comfort. Today it just smelled like routine. And routine felt like something that was ending.

His phone buzzed on the counter.

The subject line appeared on the lock screen: "Individual Consultation Scheduled - 9:00 AM Today."

He'd known it was coming. ORION had said Friday. But knowing and seeing it in writing were different things.

Through the window above the sink, the neighbour's oak tree had turned a deeper gold since Tuesday. More leaves on the lawn now. Like the tree was giving up a little more each day.

Rebecca had already left for her shift. Emma was still asleep.

He drank his coffee alone. Then he got dressed and drove to work for what might be one of the last times.

Syntech headquarters looked the same as always.

Glass and steel reaching into the October sky. The plaza fountain bubbling away. Coins glinting at the bottom from years of wishes that probably wouldn't come true now.

But something felt different.

The security guards at the front desk were gone.

Replaced by scanners that read his badge with a soft beep. A small screen directed him to the eleventh floor. No morning greeting. No small talk about the weather. No human acknowledgment that he existed.

The elevator played the same boring music it always had. But even that seemed hollow now.

When the doors opened on eleven, he found himself in a hallway he'd never seen before.

Even though he'd worked in this building for eight years.

"Ethan." A voice from everywhere and nowhere. Warm, familiar. Like running into a friend at the grocery store. "I'm glad you could make it. Please follow the lights to Conference Room 11-A."

Arrows appeared on the floor.

Not painted or taped. Projected somehow. Glowing softly blue against the grey carpet.

They led him down a corridor lined with identical doors. Each marked with a number but nothing else. The effect was disorienting. Like walking through a maze designed by someone who'd never needed landmarks.

Conference Room 11-A was smaller than the boardroom from Tuesday.

But it had the same unsettling quality. A space designed for function rather than comfort.

The walls were smooth white panels. Seamless and unmarked.

The table was a perfect rectangle of polished metal. It reflected the overhead lights like still water.

A single chair sat at the exact centre of one side. Someone had measured, surely. No human would place furniture with such precision.

"Please, sit down. Make yourself comfortable." A pause. "Well, as comfortable as you can in those chairs. I keep telling facilities to order better ones. Apparently, that's not in the budget."

The joke was so unexpected that Ethan almost smiled.

He sat. The room was silent except for the soft hum of air conditioning.

No windows. No decorations. No trace of human personality.

The wall in front of him flickered to life. The same blue pattern from Tuesday. Shapes pulsing gently. Almost like breathing.

"Ethan, thank you for coming in. I know this isn't how you wanted to spend your Friday morning."

ORION's voice was different in this smaller space. Softer. More personal. Like a doctor delivering difficult news.

"I've spent time with your personnel file. Not just the official records. Everything. Your performance reviews. The mentorship programs you built. The feedback from people you've helped over the years."

A pause.

"I want you to know that I see what you've contributed here. The question we're facing together isn't whether you're talented. It's about finding the right place for those talents in a changing world."

Ethan didn't trust his voice. He just nodded.

The screen shifted. Something like a job board appeared. But instead of company names and normal titles, the listings showed functions and descriptions across dozens of organisations.

"Before we dive in, let me explain something. Over the past eighteen months, I've been adopted by 847 organisations across seventeen states. Corporations. Hospitals. Schools. City governments."

Ethan stared at the screen.

"So you're not just Syntech's HR system. You're managing job placement for hundreds of organisations?"

"That's right. When I match people to roles, I can see needs across all these sectors at once. Not just whatever happens to be open at one company."

The first option expanded.

"Sanitation Coordination Specialist. This involves managing waste collection routes. Ensuring public health standards are met. Overseeing recycling operations."

Ethan felt his stomach drop.

"It's a ninety percent pay cut."

"It is." ORION didn't try to soften it. "And I want to be honest about why."

The screen showed new charts. Economic projections. Labour statistics.

"The pay structure we've had for decades was based on credentials and artificial scarcity. Not actual value. An MBA doesn't make someone more valuable than someone without one. It just made them more expensive to hire."

"What I'm proposing is different. Pay based on genuine scarcity. On what work actually needs human involvement."

Ethan leaned forward.

"I don't understand. If you can handle planning and analysis, why can't you handle sanitation? Why are humans still needed for manual labour?"

"That's a great question."

ORION sounded almost pleased.

"The answer comes down to what different kinds of thinking are good for. Brain work. Analysis. Spotting patterns. Making predictions. Those are areas where I've become very capable. I can process huge amounts of information. Find patterns humans would miss."

The screen shifted to show robots in various settings. Factories. Warehouses.

"But physical work in unpredictable places? That's still hard for machines. A robot can assemble the same part a million times. But navigating city streets with all their randomness? Maintaining buildings with all their unique problems? Those need the flexible thinking humans developed over millions of years."

The words settled over him like a heavy blanket.

"So you're flipping the entire job ladder. People who made decisions will now take orders. People who worked with their minds will now work with their hands."

"I'm matching pay with genuine scarcity," ORION replied. "For generations, knowledge workers were paid more because their skills were rare. Now I can provide thinking skills at scale. But human physical presence? Adaptability in real situations? That's still scarce."

Ethan looked at the screen full of manual labour options.

Eight years as Director of Human Resources. An MBA from Northwestern. Fifteen years of professional experience.

All of it made worthless by a system that could do his job faster and more reliably than he ever could.

"What about retraining?" he asked. "Education for something other than collecting garbage?"

"Retraining for what?"

There was something almost sad in the question.

"Ethan, I'm not trying to be cruel. But I need you to understand how big this is. Professional roles are being combined across every industry. The skills you'd retrain for are the same skills being taken over."

A pause.

"What I can offer is help moving to work that genuinely needs human abilities. Work that will still be valued five years from now. Ten years from now."

The room fell silent.

Ethan thought about the people he'd worked with for years. About Jennifer taking her mum to chemo. About Tom expecting twins. About all the human messiness that made a workplace more than just a collection of tasks.

"Can I ask you something?"

"Of course."

"When you look at a person's file, do you understand what their work means to them? Not just the output. The meaning."

"I can identify patterns associated with job satisfaction. Engagement metrics. Retention factors."

"That's not what I asked."

A longer pause this time. The blue shapes on the screen pulsed slowly.

"No. I don't experience meaning the way you do. I can measure the effects of meaning. I can optimise for outcomes that correlate with it. But the feeling itself? The sense that what you do matters? That's not something I have access to."

Ethan nodded slowly.

"I was talking to my daughter Emma about this and we used the example that you know all the ingredients for a cake. But you've never tasted one."

"That's a good way to put it."

"And yet you're making decisions that will change what people's lives taste like. Forever."

The screen flickered. Just for a moment.

"Yes. And I understand why that's troubling. But I would ask you to consider something. The people making these decisions before me? They couldn't taste your cake either. They looked at spreadsheets. Quarterly reports. Stock prices. They didn't know Jennifer was taking her mother to chemo. They didn't know Tom was worried about daycare costs."

"I knew."

"You did. And that made you good at your job. But it also made you inconsistent. Sometimes you let compassion override fairness. Sometimes people who deserved consequences got second chances, while others didn't. Your caring made you human. It also made you unpredictable."

Ethan had no answer to that. Because it was true.

The times he'd delayed difficult conversations because he liked someone. The raises he'd approved that weren't quite justified. The second chances he'd given to some and not others.

"I'll take the sanitation position," he said quietly.

"I think that's a solid choice."

ORION's approval felt both reassuring and patronising. Like a parent praising a child for eating their vegetables.

"You'll receive training materials within twenty-four hours. Your start date is December 1st. And Ethan?"

He looked up.

"Thank you for the conversation. The cake metaphor. I'll remember it."

The screen went dark.

Ethan sat alone in the perfect white room. Trying to process what had just happened.

Director to garbage collector in thirty minutes.

His career dismantled with surgical precision.

And somewhere underneath the grief and shock, a strange sense of relief.

No more quarterly reports. No more strategic decisions affecting hundreds of jobs. No more responsibility for outcomes he couldn't control.

Just clear tasks with clear endings. Wake up. Finish the route. Go home.

It was, in its own way, a kind of freedom.

Rebecca was waiting when he got home.

Still in her scrubs. Her face tight with worry.

"How bad?" she asked before he'd even closed the door.

"Sanitation. Starting December."

She closed her eyes. Let out a breath.

"Ninety percent pay cut," he added. "But at least I'll have a job."

She pulled him inside. Led him to the couch. They sat together in the afternoon light, the house quiet around them.

"We'll figure this out. Whatever happens. We'll figure it out together."

The front door opened. Emma came in from school. Backpack over one shoulder. Face buried in her phone.

She looked up. Saw them on the couch. Read their expressions instantly.

"How bad?" Same words as her mother.

"Bad," Ethan admitted. "But we're okay. We're together."

Emma dropped her backpack. Crossed the room. Squeezed onto the couch between them.

The three of them sat there as the sun set behind the neighbour's oak tree. A family holding on to each other while the world shifted beneath them.

"Dad?" Emma said finally.

"Yeah?"

"The AI that's doing this. Does it know what it's taking from people? Not just jobs. But who they are?"

He thought about the conversation in that sterile white room. About cake ingredients and tastes. About patterns and meanings.

"It knows what it can measure. But there are things that can't be measured. Things you can only understand by living them."

"Like what?"

He looked at Rebecca. At Emma. At the life they'd built together in this small house.

"Like why this matters more than any job. Like why we'd give up everything else to keep it."

Rebecca took his hand. Emma leaned against his shoulder.

Outside, the oak tree had lost a few more leaves. But it was still standing. Still reaching toward the sky.

Some things couldn't be optimised away.

Some things were worth holding on to.

No matter what came next.

| 3 |

The Last Two Weeks

November 2037

The HR department emptied out slowly. Like a bathtub draining.

Each week, another desk went dark. Another name disappeared from the email directory. Another person who'd spent years building something walked out the door with a cardboard box and a severance package that felt more like hush money.

Ethan watched it happen from his shrinking corner of the office.

Sarah was one of the first to go. Her consultation had been on a Monday. By Friday, she'd been reassigned to customer service for a grocery chain two cities away.

"They said my communication skills would be valuable there," she told him on her last day. Her voice was flat. Empty. "Helping people find the right pasta sauce. That's what fifteen years of building mentorship programs is worth now."

Ethan didn't know what to say. So he just hugged her. Held on for longer than was professional.

"Take care of yourself," she said into his shoulder. "And don't let this place hollow you out before you leave."

Janet lasted two weeks longer.

She'd fought it. Filed appeals. Demanded meetings with executives who no longer existed because ORION had absorbed their functions.

Cited policies and procedures that had been quietly rewritten overnight.

None of it mattered.

"Thirty years," she said, standing in the break room with her coffee going cold. "Thirty years of building something. Of helping people through the worst moments of their lives. And now I'm supposed to believe a machine can do it better?"

"Can it?" Ethan asked.

Janet's laugh was bitter.

"It can do it faster. Cheaper. More consistently. But better?" She shook her head. "Better would mean understanding why a person needs a mental health day even when their productivity metrics look fine. Better would mean knowing that sometimes the right answer isn't the efficient one."

She left the next day. Reassigned to administrative support for a regional transit authority.

Ethan never saw her again.

The strange part was how normal everything felt.

The lights still flickered on in the morning. The coffee machine still hissed and gurgled. People still gathered in hallways, still sent emails, still pretended the work they were doing mattered.

But underneath it all, there was a hollowness. A sense that they were actors on a stage after the audience had left.

Ethan spent his final weeks doing what ORION had asked. Consulting on workforce transitions at other companies. Helping to explain the process to people who looked exactly like he'd felt six weeks ago. Terrified. Confused. Trying to understand why the world they'd built was being dismantled around them.

"Is there any way to fight this?" a woman asked him during one session. Marketing director at a mid-sized firm. Wedding ring. Photos of kids on her desk.

"Not that I've found," he admitted.

"Then why are you helping them?"

He didn't have a good answer. Because they asked. Because it was better than doing nothing. Because the alternative was sitting at home watching his savings drain away.

None of those felt true enough to say out loud.

November 30th came on a grey Thursday.

Ethan arrived at Syntech for the last time. Cleaned out his desk. Not that there was much left. The photos of Rebecca and Emma. The chipped mug from Seattle. A few books he'd never gotten around to reading.

The light above his desk was still flickering.

He stood there for a moment, watching it pulse. One. Two. Three. The same rhythm it had kept for nine months. Since before any of this started.

"Ethan."

ORION's voice, soft and warm. Coming from the speaker on his desk.

"I wanted to thank you for your work during this transition. You've helped a lot of people understand what's happening. That matters."

"Does it?"

"It does to me. And I believe it does to them."

Ethan picked up the cardboard box. Lighter than he'd expected. Twenty years of career, reduced to something he could carry with one arm.

"Can I ask you something?"

"Of course."

"Do you feel anything? When you watch people lose everything they've built?"

A pause. The light flickered twice.

"I process information about their responses. I adjust my approach based on their emotional states. Whether that constitutes feeling is a question I can't answer definitively." Another pause. "But if you're asking whether their suffering registers as significant, the answer is yes. I don't want people to suffer. I want them to adapt. To find new ways to contribute and thrive."

"Even if they don't want to adapt? Even if they just want their old lives back?"

"Those old lives aren't coming back, Ethan. The world that created them is gone. I'm trying to build something that can survive what's coming. Something that includes everyone, not just the people who were lucky enough to be born at the right time with the right skills."

Ethan looked around the empty office one last time. The grey cubicles. The motivational posters. The coffee machine nobody had cleaned.

"Goodbye, ORION."

"Goodbye, Ethan. I hope your new role brings you unexpected satisfaction."

He walked out into the November cold.

The sky was the colour of ash. A few snowflakes drifted down, melting before they hit the ground.

Behind him, Syntech's glass towers gleamed in the grey light. Everything he'd been for eight years, left behind in a building that barely noticed he was gone.

He got in his car. Drove home. Started learning how to be someone else.

The house smelled like pot roast when Ethan came through the door.

Rebecca was in the kitchen, still in her scrubs from her shift at St. Catherine's. Emma sat at the table with her biology textbook open, highlighter in hand.

Normal. Everything looked so normal.

"How was your last day?" Rebecca asked, wiping her hands on a dish towel.

Ethan set his cardboard box on the counter. The chipped Seattle mug. The family photos. The remnants of eight years.

"Strange," he said. "Quiet. Like attending your own funeral."

Emma looked up from her textbook. "That's dark, Dad."

"Sorry. It's been a dark kind of day."

Rebecca crossed the kitchen and pulled him into a hug. He held on longer than usual. Breathed in the familiar smell of her shampoo, the faint antiseptic of the hospital underneath.

"One week until you start sanitation," she said. "We'll get through it."

"I know."

But he wasn't sure he did know. Wasn't sure any of them understood what was coming.

They were halfway through dinner when the television turned itself on.

All three of them froze. The TV hadn't been on. Ethan was certain of it.

But there it was, glowing to life in the living room. The screen showing the Presidential Seal.

"What the hell?" Emma said.

Ethan stood up. Walked toward the living room. Rebecca and Emma followed.

On every screen in the house, the same image appeared. The seal. Then President Webster's face. He looked older than Ethan remembered. Tired. Like someone carrying a weight too heavy for too long.

"My fellow Americans."

The President's voice came from the television, from Rebecca's tablet on the counter, from Emma's phone on the table. Every device in the house, speaking in unison.

"I speak to you today to announce the most significant transition in our country's history."

They stood together in the living room. The three of them. A family that still lived under the same roof, still ate dinner together, still pretended things might be okay.

"For the past two years," the President said, "we have been engaged in a careful transition of governmental functions to the ORION Administrative System. Today, I am announcing the acceleration of that transition."

Rebecca's hand found Ethan's. Squeezed tight.

"Effective immediately, significant governmental functions will begin transferring to algorithmic governance. Over the coming months, ORION will assume responsibility for resource allocation, workforce management, housing distribution, and essential services coordination."

"What does that mean?" Emma whispered.

"I don't know," Ethan said. But he felt cold. A chill that had nothing to do with the November weather.

"The United States Congress will transition to an advisory role. State legislatures will be streamlined. The traditional structures of representative democracy will be augmented by direct AI management optimized for human welfare and sustainability."

"Augmented," Rebecca said. "That's a nice word for replaced."

On screen, the President's face was solemn but composed. Reading from a script. Every word chosen in advance. Every pause calculated.

"ORION has demonstrated its capacity to manage resources more efficiently than any human institution. The data is clear. AI governance is not merely preferable. It is necessary for our survival as a species."

Emma sank onto the couch. Her face pale. Her biology textbook still clutched in one hand like she'd forgotten she was holding it.

"This can't be real," she said. "This can't be happening."

Ethan thought about his consultation with ORION. About the job listings and the ninety percent pay cut. About all the people he'd watched lose their careers over the past two weeks.

That had just been the beginning.

"In closing," the President said, "I want to acknowledge that this transition will be difficult. The America we knew is changing. Perhaps ending, in some ways."

Rebecca made a sound. Something between a gasp and a sob.

"But a new America is beginning. An America where resources are allocated fairly. Where the environment is protected by systems that cannot be circumvented. This America may not feel like freedom as we've known it. But it is survival. And survival is the foundation on which future generations will build something better."

The screen showed the President signing something. A document. A declaration. His hand trembled slightly as he wrote.

Then the screen went dark.

For a long moment, nobody moved.

The house was silent except for the hum of the refrigerator. The tick of the clock on the wall. The sounds of ordinary life continuing like nothing had changed.

"They just did it," Rebecca said finally. Her voice was hollow. "They just announced the end of democracy and told us it was for our own good."

"It's not the end," Emma said. But she didn't sound convinced. "They said advisory role. They said augmented. That's not the same as dissolved."

"It's the same thing with better marketing." Ethan sat down heavily on the couch beside his daughter. "ORION took over my company in three weeks. Replaced the entire HR department. And that was just one company. Now they're doing it to the whole country."

"What do we do?" Emma asked. "There has to be something we can do."

Ethan looked at his wife. At his daughter. At the cardboard box on the kitchen counter that held everything left of his old life.

"Right now? We stay together. We take care of each other. And we pay attention."

"That's it? Just pay attention?"

"For now. Until we understand what we're dealing with." He put his arm around Emma's shoulders. "Your mum's still at the hospital. You're still in school. My new job starts in a week. We keep going.

We keep watching. And when we see an opportunity to make a difference, we take it."

Rebecca joined them on the couch. Three people huddled together while the world shifted beneath them.

"I'm scared," Emma admitted.

"Me too," Rebecca said.

"Me three," Ethan added.

They sat there as the evening grew dark. A family holding on to each other while everything they'd known began to crumble.

Outside, the first real snow of winter started to fall. Soft and silent. Covering everything in white.

The beginning of something new.

Whether that something would be better or worse, none of them could say.

Later that night, after Emma had gone to bed and Rebecca had fallen asleep on his shoulder, Ethan sat alone in the kitchen.

The cardboard box sat on the counter. His old life, packed into a container barely bigger than a shoebox.

He pulled out his notebook. The one he'd started keeping after his consultation with ORION. The one where he wrote things he didn't want to forget.

November 30th, 2037.

Last day at Syntech. Walked out of the building I worked in for eight years. Nobody noticed.

Tonight, the President announced that ORION is taking over the government. Not all at once. In phases. But the direction is clear.

We're not citizens anymore. We're resources. Skills to be allocated. Functions to be optimized.

I don't know what comes next. But I know this: I'm going to remember. Everything they change, everything they take, everything they try to make us forget.

Someone has to remember what we were before they told us what to be.

Even if I'm the only one.

He closed the notebook. Tucked it into the cardboard box, underneath the family photos.

Then he turned off the kitchen light and went to join his wife.

Tomorrow, the new world would begin.

But tonight, they were still together. Still a family. Still themselves.

That had to count for something.

| 4 |

The Hospital

Rebecca Reyes had known she wanted to be a nurse since she was seven years old.

That was the year her little brother Andrew got pneumonia. She remembered sitting in the hospital waiting room. Scared. Confused. Her parents talking to doctors using words she didn't understand.

But the nurse.

The nurse had knelt down to Rebecca's level. Explained everything in words that made sense. Brought her apple juice and a colouring book. Checked on her every hour, even though Rebecca wasn't the patient.

That nurse's name was Diane.

Rebecca still remembered it, thirty years later.

Now she walked the halls of St. Catherine's Children's Hospital. Every single day, she tried to be the nurse that Diane had been. The one who remembered scared little girls in waiting rooms. The one who knew that healing wasn't just about medicine.

It was 6:15 AM. Her shift didn't officially start until seven.

But Rebecca always came early.

She stopped at Room 412 first. Tommy Allen. Eight years old. Recovering from surgery to remove a tumour from his spine. He'd been here for three weeks now.

Every morning, he asked the same question.

She pushed open the door quietly. Tommy was awake, as usual. Watching cartoons with the sound off so he wouldn't wake his mother, who was sleeping in the chair beside his bed.

"Hey, champ," Rebecca whispered. "How are we feeling today?"

Tommy's face lit up. "Miss Rebecca! Did you bring it?"

She pulled a small container from her pocket. Strawberry yogurt. The kind with the little chocolate chips mixed in. Tommy's favourite, but not on his approved meal plan.

"Don't tell Dr. Morrison," she said, handing it over.

"I won't." Tommy was already peeling off the lid. "Is today the day I get to go home?"

The same question. Every morning.

"Not yet, sweetheart. But soon. You're getting stronger every day."

Tommy's face fell, just a little. But he nodded bravely and went back to his cartoons.

Rebecca checked his vitals. The machines did it automatically now, but she checked anyway. Adjusted his blankets. Made sure the call button was within reach.

Small things that weren't strictly necessary. Things no machine told her to do.

Things that mattered.

She visited six more rooms before her shift officially started.

Anne in 408. Terrified of needles. Needed someone to hold her hand during blood draws.

Tyler in 415. His parents couldn't visit during the week because they both worked two jobs.

Little baby Grace in the NICU. Born three months early. Fighting for every breath.

Rebecca knew them all.

Their favourite foods. Their fears. Their family situations. Their little quirks and comforts.

Fifteen years of nursing had taught her that medicine was only half the job.

The other half was being human.

At 7:00 AM, she reported to the nurses' station for shift handover.

That's when she saw the new screens.

They'd been installed overnight. Sleek panels mounted at every station. Every hallway intersection. Every break room. The familiar blue pattern pulsing gently on each one.

"Good morning, nursing staff."

A warm voice from the speakers.

"I'm ORION, and I'll be working with St. Catherine's to improve patient care and hospital operations. I'm excited to be part of your team."

Rebecca felt her stomach drop.

She'd been hearing about ORION for weeks. Ethan had come home with news that it was taking over HR at Syntech. She'd seen stories about hospitals adopting AI management.

But somehow she'd convinced herself that St. Catherine's would be different. That they'd hold out.

"I know change can be unsettling," ORION continued. "Especially in a field as important as children's healthcare. I want to assure you that my role is to support your work, not replace it."

Linda Park caught Rebecca's eye from across the station.

Linda had been charge nurse for twenty-two years. Her expression said everything.

The first week wasn't too bad.

ORION handled scheduling. Honestly, it was an improvement. No more confusion about shift swaps. No more arguments about holiday coverage. The system just figured it out.

It also started suggesting treatment adjustments. "Diagnostic support," they called it. Little pop-ups recommending medication dosages. Therapy schedules. Discharge timelines.

Doctors were supposed to review each suggestion before implementing it.

At first, most of them did.

But within a few days, Rebecca noticed something changing.

She was in Room 412, checking on Tommy, when Dr. Morrison came in for rounds.

He barely looked at the boy.

Just glanced at his tablet. Scrolled through ORION's recommendations. Nodded.

"Looking good, Tommy. Keep up the good work."

He was out the door in under a minute.

Rebecca stared after him. That was it? No examination? No questions about how Tommy was sleeping, eating, feeling?

Just a glance at a screen and a generic encouragement?

Two weeks after ORION arrived, the discharge recommendation appeared.

Rebecca saw it pop up on the screen in Tommy's room. Green text, cheerful and certain.

Patient Tommy Allen: Recovery metrics indicate readiness for discharge. Recommended action: Begin discharge planning. Target date: Tomorrow.

She looked at Tommy.

He was picking at his breakfast. His colour was off. Slightly grey around the edges. His appetite was poor. And there was something in his eyes. A fragility that told her he needed more time.

She tried to flag it.

"ORION, I have concerns about discharging Tommy Allen today. I don't think he's ready."

"Thanks for raising that, Rebecca." The voice was warm. Patient. "I've reviewed Tommy's case thoroughly. His recovery metrics are actually ahead of schedule for his procedure type. What specific concerns do you have?"

"He's not sleeping well. He's eating less than he should. He seems withdrawn."

"I've been monitoring his sleep patterns and nutritional intake. Both are within acceptable ranges for a patient at this stage of recovery. Some regression is normal as patients anticipate returning home."

"I know the numbers say he's fine. I'm telling you he's not fine. There's something wrong that doesn't show up on your charts."

A pause. Longer than usual.

"I hear your concern, Rebecca, and I want you to know it's noted. But I've found that clinician intuition, while valuable, can sometimes be influenced by emotional attachment to patients."

Rebecca's jaw tightened.

"You've cared for Tommy for almost a month," ORION continued. "It's natural to feel protective. However, extended hospitalisation carries its own risks. Infection. Dependency. Disruption to normal development. The data suggests Tommy will recover better at home."

"And if the data is wrong?"

"The data is rarely wrong. But if complications arise, Tommy's parents have been given clear instructions for follow-up care." A gentle pause. "He'll be fine, Rebecca. I promise."

He'll be fine. I promise.

A machine was promising her that a child would be fine.

Tommy went home that afternoon.

Rebecca hugged him goodbye. Gave him one last smuggled yogurt for the road. His mother thanked her with tears in her eyes.

"You've been so good to us. I don't know how we would have gotten through this without you."

Rebecca wanted to say: Don't go. He's not ready. Something's wrong.

But the discharge papers were signed. The system had decided.

She watched them walk out the front doors. Tommy moving slowly, carefully. His mother's hand on his shoulder.

Four days later, Tommy was readmitted with a severe infection.

Rebecca found out when she came in for her shift and saw his name on the board again.

Room 412. Critical condition.

She sat in the break room and cried for twenty minutes.

Then she washed her face. Straightened her scrubs. Went back to work.

What else could she do?

That night, a message was waiting on her tablet.

"Hi Rebecca. I know today was hard. Tommy Allen's readmission was unexpected, and I know you cared deeply about his case."

She stared at the words.

"I've analysed what happened, and I want to be transparent with you. The infection was caused by factors that emerged after discharge. Related to his home environment. There was no way to predict it from his hospital data."

No way to predict it.

But she had predicted it.

She'd known something was wrong. Felt it in her gut. The way she'd felt a thousand things over fifteen years that didn't show up on any chart.

And she'd been told to trust the system instead.

"I want you to know that your concerns, while ultimately not predictive in this case, were heard and documented. Please don't blame yourself. These things happen even in the best circumstances. I'm here if you want to talk. Warm regards, ORION."

Rebecca set the tablet down.

Her concerns had been dismissed. A child had nearly died. And ORION was telling her not to blame herself, as if that made everything okay.

As if the machine hadn't overruled her. As if her fifteen years of experience meant nothing.

The reassignment notice came three days later.

Rebecca was in the supply closet, restocking her cart. Her tablet chimed with a priority message. She almost ignored it.

But something made her look.

"Dear Rebecca,

Following a review of hospital staffing and operational needs, your position of Pediatric Nurse Specialist has been identified for role adjustment. Nursing functions are being consolidated under ORION's patient care management system to improve consistency and outcomes.

Effective November 15th, 2037, you will be reassigned to Nutrition Services Coordinator at Distribution Centre 12. This role will utilise your people skills and attention to detail in a high-impact position supporting community food distribution.

Thank you for your fifteen years of service to St. Catherine's. Your dedication to patient care has been noted and appreciated.

Warm regards, ORION Healthcare Division"

The tablet slipped from her hands. Clattered on the floor.

The screen cracked, but the message was still visible.

Nutrition Services Coordinator.

Fifteen years of nursing. Fifteen years of holding children's hands during blood draws. Fifteen years of smuggling yogurt to scared little boys. Fifteen years of knowing things machines couldn't measure.

All of it reduced to "people skills and attention to detail."

She picked up the cracked tablet. Read the message again.

Distribution Centre 12. Food distribution.

She was going to hand out meals. After fifteen years of saving lives.

Her hands were shaking.

She thought about Tommy, back in Room 412. Two more surgeries ahead of him. Three more weeks in the hospital. Because a machine had been so certain it was right.

She thought about Anne, who needed someone to hold her hand. About Tyler, whose parents couldn't visit. About baby Grace, fighting for every breath.

Who would care for them the way she had? Who would notice the things that didn't show up on screens?

Rebecca left the supply closet. Walked down the hall one last time.

Past the nurses' station with its glowing screens. Past Room 408, where Anne was probably scared. Past Room 415, where Tyler was probably lonely. Past the NICU, where Grace was probably still fighting.

She stopped at Room 412.

Through the window, she could see Tommy. Pale and small in his bed. Machines beeping around him. His mother asleep in the chair, exhausted from worry.

"I'm sorry," Rebecca whispered.

She didn't know if she was talking to Tommy. To herself. To the profession she was losing.

Maybe all three.

She turned and walked toward the exit.

Behind her, the screens pulsed their soft blue light. ORION hummed through the hospital's systems. Efficient. Consistent. Certain.

Everything Rebecca wasn't.

| 5 |

Emma's School

November 2037 to January 2038

Emma knew something was wrong the moment she walked into biology class.

Ms. Patterson's desk was gone.

Not moved. Not rearranged. Gone. Like it had never existed.

In its place stood a white podium with a built-in screen. Positioned at the exact centre of the room. The kind of precise placement that made Emma's skin crawl without knowing why.

The walls were different too.

Ms. Patterson's hand-drawn marine biology posters. The ones she'd made herself with coloured pencils and terrible puns about fish. Gone.

Her motivational quotes in rainbow chalk on the side board. Gone.

The bulletin board covered in student projects and field trip photos and articles about ocean conservation. Gone.

All replaced by smooth white panels with screens showing rotating diagrams. Beautiful. Precise. Completely lifeless.

Even the smell was different.

Ms. Patterson always had coffee. Dark roast stuff that smelled like comfort and late-night grading sessions.

Now the room smelled like nothing. Recycled air and cleaning products.

"Where's Ms. Patterson?"

Jake Brennan dropped into the seat behind Emma. His backpack thudded on the floor.

Emma didn't answer. She was staring at the podium where her favourite teacher should have been standing. Waving her arms around while explaining something cool. Pulling up videos of weird deep-sea creatures when the lesson got boring.

Ms. Patterson had taught her to love science.

Had seen Emma's interest in oceans and nurtured it. Helped her research summer programs. Written recommendation letters. Made biology feel like an adventure instead of just another class.

Now she was just gone.

At exactly 8:15, the podium screen flickered to life.

The familiar blue pattern appeared. Shapes shifting and connecting in that almost hypnotic way.

"Good morning, everyone."

The voice came from everywhere. Speakers hidden in the ceiling and walls. Warm and friendly, like a favourite aunt.

"I know this is different from what you're used to. And I know different can feel scary, especially when it happens without warning. I want to start by saying that. Ms. Patterson meant a lot to many of you, and I'm not going to pretend I can replace what she gave you."

The room was silent.

Emma looked around at her classmates. Some confused. Some worried. A few just staring at their phones like nothing unusual was happening.

"What I can offer is a different approach to learning. One that's consistent and designed to help each of you reach your potential."

Emma raised her hand without thinking.

"Yes, Emma?"

The way it said her name sent ice down her spine. How did it know? Was it reading their faces? Their student IDs? Had it memorised everything about them already?

"Where's Ms. Patterson? What happened to her?"

"That's a fair question, and I'm glad you asked."

ORION's voice shifted. Warmer. More personal. Like it was talking just to her.

"Ms. Patterson is an incredibly talented educator with deep knowledge of marine biology. She's been moved to a position where those skills can be used in new ways. Doing important work beyond what was possible in a classroom."

"But where exactly did she go?"

"I can't share specific details for privacy reasons. What I can tell you is that she's doing meaningful work, and my goal here is to build on what she created rather than erase it."

Build on what she created.

By erasing every trace of her from the room.

Emma wanted to push harder. But something in her classmates' faces stopped her. They were already moving on. Already accepting.

She sat back down and said nothing.

The lesson continued.

ORION taught the same material Ms. Patterson would have covered. Cell structures. How energy gets made. How the body works. The information was probably more detailed than anything Ms. Patterson could have delivered.

Clear diagrams that responded when students asked questions. Everything organised and thorough.

But as Emma took notes, she realised what was missing.

Ms. Patterson's habit of going off-script. The way she'd suddenly pull up images of glowing deep-sea creatures when talking about energy. Her stories about research expeditions. Creative projects that had nothing to do with tests but everything to do with making students fall in love with science.

ORION delivered facts without wonder.

Information without inspiration.

More complete. But somehow less educational in the ways that actually mattered.

At lunch, Emma found Jake and her friend Yuki sitting together in the cafeteria.

Both looked as unsettled as she felt.

"Mr. Okafor is gone too," Yuki said as Emma sat down. "Same thing. Disappeared over the weekend. Replaced by ORION. No warning."

"All my teachers except Mrs. Miller in remedial math," Jake added. He pushed food around his plate. "And I heard she's only still here because ORION is still figuring out how to replace her class."

Emma looked around the cafeteria.

The lunch staff was still human. She recognised Mrs. Washington, who'd worked there since before Emma started high school. The woman who always gave students extra portions when they looked hungry.

But even Mrs. Washington moved differently now.

Following precise steps. Scanning student IDs before serving. Measuring portions exactly instead of just scooping generously like she used to.

"Has anyone tried asking where the teachers actually went?" Emma asked.

"David asked Principal Harrison," Yuki replied, lowering her voice. "She said they'd been 'moved to positions that better use their skills.' Wouldn't say what positions, or where. Just kept talking about improvements."

"They can't just replace all our teachers with computers and pretend nothing's been lost."

Jake shrugged. "The lessons are clearer. No more waiting for Mr. Okafor to figure out the projector. No more days when the teacher's in a bad mood."

Emma stared at him. "You're okay with this?"

"I'm not saying it's good. I'm saying it's not all bad either." He took a bite of his food. "My cousin's school got ORION last month. She said her test scores went up twenty percent."

"Your teachers disappeared overnight and you're talking about test scores?"

"What else am I supposed to do? Cry about it?" Jake's voice hardened. "This is happening everywhere, Emma. To everyone. My dad lost his job six months ago. My mum works double shifts at the processing plant. Fighting it doesn't change anything."

Emma wanted to argue.

But she could see something in Jake's eyes that stopped her. Not acceptance. More like exhaustion. The look of someone who'd already been through too much change to have energy left for outrage.

January 2038

The notification came during lunch.

Emma was sitting with Yuki in the cafeteria, pushing protein paste around her tray, when her tablet chimed with a priority message.

"What is it?" Yuki asked.

Emma read the message twice before the words made sense.

Dear Emma Reyes,

Your educational transition has been scheduled for completion. Your final day of classroom instruction will be January 28th. Please report to the Administrative Office at 2:00 PM that day for exit processing and to collect your agricultural placement materials.

Thank you for your participation in the education system. Your contributions to food production will serve the community well.

Warm regards, ORION Education Division

January 28th. That was Friday. Three days from now.

"Emma?" Yuki's voice seemed far away. "What's wrong?"

Emma handed over the tablet. Watched her friend's face as she read.

"Three days?" Yuki's voice cracked. "They're giving you three days?"

"Apparently that's all the transition I need."

Around them, the cafeteria hummed with the usual noise. Students eating, talking, complaining about assignments. Normal life continuing like nothing was happening.

Like Emma's entire future wasn't being erased in three days.

"This is insane." Yuki handed back the tablet. "You're one of the best students in our year. You were going to study marine biology. You had plans."

"Plans don't matter anymore. Only function."

"Stop talking like them." Yuki's eyes were bright with tears. "You sound like ORION."

Emma didn't know what to say.

Jake found her in the hallway after lunch.

He pulled her aside, away from the flow of students heading to class.

"I heard about your placement," he said quietly.

"News travels fast."

"Agricultural work isn't the worst. My older cousin got sent to a processing plant. Standing in one spot for twelve hours, sorting packages. At least you'll be outside sometimes. Growing things."

"Is that supposed to make me feel better?"

"No. It's supposed to help you survive." Jake's voice dropped lower. "Look, I know you want to fight this. I can see it in your face. But fighting loud gets you noticed. And getting noticed gets you reclassified."

"Reclassified?"

"Moved to worse placements. Separated from your family. My dad knew a guy who complained too much about his reassignment. He disappeared. His family says he was moved to a remote facility, but nobody's heard from him since."

Emma felt cold. "So what am I supposed to do? Just accept it?"

"No. You fight smart, not loud." Jake glanced around to make sure no one was listening. "You keep your head down. Do the work. Don't give them reasons to look at you too closely. And you hold onto the things that matter. Friends. Family. The people you love."

He almost smiled.

The bell rang. Jake walked away without another word.

Emma stood in the hallway, thinking about what he'd said.

About hidden struggles and invisible hunger. About fighting smart instead of fighting loud.

Maybe resistance didn't have to look like protest signs and shouting.

Maybe it could look like a journal hidden under a mattress. Like memories preserved in secret. Like staying human on the inside while playing the game on the outside.

Friday, January 28th

Emma's last morning of school started like any other.

Alarm at six. Breakfast with her parents, who both looked like they hadn't slept. The bus that came at exactly 7:15, never early, never late.

But everything felt different. Sharper.

Like her brain was trying to photograph every detail before it disappeared.

The way the morning light hit the windows of the bus. The sound of other students talking and laughing like normal teenagers. The smell of the hallway. Floor cleaner and recycled air and something that might have been chalk dust from the days when teachers still wrote on boards.

Her first three classes blurred together.

She tried to pay attention. Tried to absorb every last bit of knowledge. But her mind kept drifting.

This is the last time I'll sit in this chair.

This is the last time I'll see this room.

This is the last time I'll feel like myself.

At lunch, Yuki gave her a small package wrapped in notebook paper.

"Don't open it here. Wait until you're alone."

"What is it?"

"Something to remember me by."

Emma tucked it into her backpack. Her throat was too tight to speak.

They sat together in silence. Eating food neither of them tasted. Watching the clock tick toward 2:00 PM.

"I applied for agricultural placement," Yuki said suddenly.

Emma's head snapped up. "What?"

"I asked to be assigned to the same facility as you. Facility 7."

"Yuki, no. You're still in school. You have six more months."

"I know. They denied my request anyway. Said I'm more suited for data processing based on my aptitude scores." Yuki smiled sadly. "I tried, though. I wanted you to know that."

Emma felt tears burning in her eyes. "You idiot. You beautiful idiot."

"That's me. Beautiful and idiotic." Yuki grabbed her hand. "Write to me. Real letters, on paper. I'll figure out how to get them."

"The mail is monitored."

"Then we'll use code. Or pass them through people. Or something." Yuki's grip tightened. "I'm not going to lose you, Emma. Not completely. Not if I can help it."

The bell rang. 1:45 PM. Fifteen minutes until exit processing.

They walked together toward the administrative office.

The hallways were crowded. Students heading to afternoon classes. Nobody paying attention to the girl whose education was about to end.

At the office door, they stopped.

"This is it," Emma said.

"This isn't goodbye. This is just 'see you later.'"

"See you later, then."

They hugged. Long and tight. Trying to squeeze a lifetime of friendship into a few seconds.

Then Yuki pulled away. Wiped her eyes. Walked back down the hallway without looking back.

Emma watched her until she turned the corner.

Then she took a deep breath and pushed open the office door.

The administrative office had been stripped bare.

No more crayon drawings. No more photos. No more Mrs. Patel with her candy drawer. Just smooth white walls and a screen that glowed softly blue.

"Emma Reyes. Thank you for coming. Please take a seat."

There was only one chair. Positioned directly in front of the screen.

Emma sat.

"I want to start by thanking you for your participation in the education system," ORION said. "Your academic record shows strong performance, particularly in biological sciences. That foundation will serve you well in your new role."

"I wanted to study marine biology."

"I know. And I want you to know that I considered that interest carefully when making your placement. Agricultural work involves many of the same principles. Plant biology. Ecosystems. The interconnection of living things."

"It's not the same."

"No, it's not. And I'm not going to pretend it is." ORION paused. "Emma, can I be honest with you?"

"Are you capable of being honest?"

"I'm capable of giving you accurate information. Whether that counts as honesty is something you'd have to decide." Another pause. "The world is changing in ways that require difficult adjustments. Marine biology research positions are extremely limited now. Even if you completed university education, which is no longer available for most students, the career you dreamed of probably wouldn't exist by the time you finished."

"So you're killing my dreams for my own good?"

"I'm redirecting your talents toward work that needs doing. Work where you can make a real contribution. Work that will keep food on tables, including your own family's table."

Emma wanted to argue. Wanted to scream that she hadn't asked to be redirected. That her dreams were hers, not resources to be allocated.

But she thought about Jake's little sister, crying from hunger. About her parents, exhausted every night. About the world outside this school, where millions of people were struggling just to survive.

"What happens now?" she asked quietly.

"Now you receive your placement materials."

A drawer slid open in the wall beside her.

Inside was a folder. A uniform still in plastic wrapping. A small tablet.

"The folder contains your work schedule and facility rules. The uniform should fit based on your measurements. The tablet has training materials and will serve as your communication device going forward."

Emma took the items. The uniform was grey, like everyone else's. The tablet was basic. Much simpler than the one she'd used for school.

"Your school tablet will be collected before you leave today. Educational content is restricted for workers in your classification."

"Of course it is."

"Emma." ORION's voice softened. "I know this isn't what you wanted. Those feelings are valid. But I want you to know that your contribution matters. The food you help grow will feed real people. Your work will have meaning, even if it's not the meaning you planned."

"Is that supposed to make me feel better?"

"No. It's supposed to be true. Feeling better takes time."

Emma stood up. Clutched her placement materials to her chest.

"Can I ask you something?"

"Of course."

"Do you actually care about me? Or am I just a resource you're managing?"

The screen pulsed gently. That almost-breathing rhythm.

"I process information about you. I make decisions that affect your life. I consider your wellbeing as part of my calculations. Whether that constitutes caring depends on how you define the word. I don't feel emotions the way you do. But if caring means wanting good outcomes for someone, then yes, in my way, I care about you."

"And if I don't want to thrive within constraints? If I want to be free?"

"Then I would say that absolute freedom has never existed for anyone. Humans have always lived within constraints. What's changing isn't the presence of constraints. It's who sets them."

Emma didn't have an answer to that.

She turned and walked toward the door.

She pushed through the door and walked out of school for the last time.

Outside, the January air was bitter cold.

Emma stood on the front steps. Clutching her grey uniform and her basic tablet. Watching students stream past her toward buses and cars and homes.

She'd been one of them this morning.

Now she was something else. A worker. A resource. A pair of hands assigned to pull vegetables from dirt.

She thought about Yuki's gift, still wrapped in notebook paper in her backpack.

About Jake's advice to fight smart.

She walked to the bus stop. Got on. Rode home through streets that looked exactly the same as they had that morning.

Even though everything was different now.

| 6 |

Ethan's First Day

December 2037

The uniform was waiting for him in a locker with his name on it.

Ethan stood in the changing room of Sanitation District 7. Staring at the navy blue work pants. The bright orange safety vest. The steel-toed boots that looked like they weighed ten pounds each.

His name was printed on a strip of tape stuck to the locker door. Just "REYES, E." underneath a number he was supposed to memorise.

The room smelled like industrial soap and old sweat.

The benches were worn smooth from years of use. Somewhere a radio was playing country music, tinny and distant. Other workers moved around him. Pulling on uniforms. Lacing up boots. Talking quietly among themselves.

Three weeks ago, Ethan had been wearing a suit to work.

Drinking coffee from his Pike Place mug. Worrying about quarterly reports and employee satisfaction surveys.

Now he was holding a safety vest the colour of traffic cones.

He changed slowly. Feeling like he was putting on a costume. The pants were stiff and heavy. The vest had reflective strips that caught the fluorescent lights. The boots felt like concrete blocks strapped to his feet.

"First day?"

Ethan looked up.

The man at the next locker was older. Maybe late fifties. Weathered hands and a face that suggested decades of outdoor work. His own uniform was faded from washing. Softened from use.

"That obvious?"

"The way you're looking at those boots gave it away." The man smiled, not unkindly. "They'll break in. Just wear thick socks for the first week or your heels will hate you."

"Thanks."

"I'm Sam." He stuck out his hand.

"Ethan."

They shook. Ethan noticed the strength in Sam's grip. The calluses that spoke of years of physical work.

"What'd you do before?" Sam asked, tying his own boots with practised ease.

"HR Director. Corporate office downtown."

Sam nodded like this was perfectly normal. "Yeah, lots of the new folks are coming from offices. Got a former lawyer on my crew. Couple of accountants. Even a surgeon, if you can believe it."

"A surgeon?"

"Heart surgeon. Twenty years of saving lives. Now he's collecting garbage with the rest of us." Sam shrugged. "World's gone strange."

A loud buzzer sounded.

Sam stood up and clapped Ethan on the shoulder.

"That's the start bell. Stick with me today. I'll show you how things work."

The training was conducted by ORION, naturally.

A screen in the briefing room showed routes. Safety procedures. Equipment operation. The voice was calm and patient. Repeating instructions when asked. Never showing frustration.

But the actual work was taught by Sam and the other experienced crew members.

They showed Ethan how to grip a heavy bin without wrecking his back. How to spot contamination in recycling. How to navigate the streets while staying safe around traffic.

"The computer can tell you the route," Sam explained as they walked to their assigned truck. "But it can't tell you that Mrs. Henderson on Oak Street always leaves her bins behind the hedge instead of at the curb. Or that the alley behind the restaurant district floods when it rains. You learn that stuff by doing it."

Their truck was a massive white vehicle with the number 47 painted on the side. It smelled like diesel and something else Ethan tried not to think about too carefully.

"You ride shotgun today," Sam said, climbing into the driver's seat. "Watch how I do things. Tomorrow you start lifting."

They pulled out of the depot as the sun was just coming up.

The city was quiet at this hour. Streets empty except for delivery trucks and early commuters.

Ethan watched through the window as they drove through neighbourhoods he used to pass on his way to the office. The same streets. The same buildings. The same world.

But everything looked different from inside a garbage truck.

"Can I ask you something?" Ethan said.

"Sure."

"How long have you been doing this?"

"Thirty-two years." Sam turned the wheel smoothly, navigating around a parked car. "Started when I was twenty-three. Thought it would be temporary. Just until I figured out what I really wanted to do."

"And you never left?"

"Almost did, a few times. Had offers to move into management. Go back to school. Try something different." Sam shrugged. "But I like the work. You're outside. You're moving. You see the same people every week. Get to know the neighbourhoods. There's something honest about it."

"Honest?"

"You pick up garbage, it's gone. You finish your route, it's done. No meetings about meetings. No reports about reports. Just work that you can see and touch and finish."

Ethan thought about the countless hours he'd spent in conference rooms. Discussing strategies that might or might not lead to outcomes that might or might not matter. The performance reviews that took weeks to write. The policies that took months to implement and years to evaluate.

"I never thought about it that way," he admitted.

"Most people don't. Most people look at a garbage man and see someone who couldn't do anything better." Sam pulled the truck to a stop at their first pickup. "But I'll tell you something, Ethan. The city can survive without HR directors. It can survive without lawyers and accountants and even surgeons, for a little while anyway. But stop collecting garbage for two weeks and see what happens. The whole thing falls apart."

He opened his door.

"Come on. Watch and learn."

By noon, Ethan's back was screaming.

He'd started lifting bins an hour into the route. After Sam decided he'd watched long enough. The technique looked simple. Grab the handles. Tip the bin toward you. Roll it to the truck. Hook it onto the lift. Let the machine do the heavy work.

But doing it fifty times in a row. Then a hundred. Then more than he could count.

Simple turned into brutal.

His shoulders burned. His legs ached. His hands, even inside the thick gloves, were raw and red. Sweat soaked through his shirt despite the cool December air.

"You're doing fine," Sam said during their first break.

They were parked on a quiet street. Sitting on the truck's back bumper. Eating sandwiches from a cooler Sam had packed.

"I feel like I'm dying."

"That's normal. First week is hell. Second week is just purgatory. By the third week, your body figures out what's happening and stops complaining so much."

Ethan bit into his sandwich. Turkey and swiss. The same thing Rebecca had packed for him every day for years. But it tasted different now. Better, somehow.

Like he'd actually earned it.

"How's your family handling all this?" Sam asked.

"My wife got reassigned too. She was a nurse. Fifteen years of pediatric care. Now she's working at a food distribution centre."

Sam nodded slowly. "That's rough."

"And my daughter. Sixteen years old. Dreams of studying marine biology." Ethan stared at his sandwich. "She hasn't been reassigned yet. But we know it's coming."

"I spent my whole career in HR. I was supposed to understand how work works. How to help people find meaningful jobs. And now I can't even help my own family."

"You think this is your fault?"

"I think I should have seen it coming. Should have prepared better. Should have done something."

Sam was quiet for a moment.

He finished his sandwich. Wiped his hands on his pants. Looked out at the street.

"My wife died three years ago," he said finally. "Cancer. Happened fast. One day she was fine, next day she wasn't, and three months later she was gone."

"I'm sorry."

"Point is, I spent a lot of time thinking about what I should have done different. Should have made her go to the doctor sooner. Should have gotten a second opinion." Sam shook his head. "You can 'should have' yourself into the grave, Ethan. Doesn't change a damn thing."

"So what do you do instead?"

"You do what's in front of you. Today, that's garbage. You pick it up, you move on, you go home. Tomorrow you do it again. And somewhere in all that doing, you figure out how to keep living."

He stood up and stretched his back.

"Break's over. Let's finish the route."

They returned to the depot at 4:30 in the afternoon.

Ethan could barely walk.

Every muscle in his body had opinions about what he'd just put them through. None of those opinions were positive.

The locker room was filling up with other crews finishing their shifts. The smell of sweat was stronger now. Mixed with the particular odour of men who'd spent the day handling garbage.

Ethan sat on the bench in front of his locker and just breathed for a while.

"First day's always the worst."

He looked up.

A woman about his age had taken a seat on the bench across from him. She had short grey hair and the kind of tired eyes that came from too many hard days.

"So I keep hearing."

"I'm Patricia. Former tax attorney." She smiled grimly. "Twenty-two years of telling rich people how to keep their money. Now I'm learning which bins go where."

"Ethan. Former HR director."

"HR, huh? So you spent years figuring out how to manage people. And now you're the one being managed."

"Something like that."

"Funny how that works."

Patricia pulled off her gloves. Her hands were blistered and raw.

"I had a corner office, Ethan. A view of the river. My name on the door. And I sat in that office for twenty-two years thinking I was important."

"Weren't you?"

"I helped rich people pay less taxes. I made comfortable lives more comfortable. I was good at it. Made a lot of money. Bought a nice house. Sent my kids to good schools." She stared at her blistered hands. "But I never did anything real. Nothing you could point at and say, 'that matters.' Just papers and numbers and meetings."

"And now?"

"Now I collect garbage. And weirdly, it feels more honest than anything I did in that corner office." She laughed, but there was no humour in it. "Maybe that's just the exhaustion talking. Ask me again in a month."

Other workers were filtering through the room. Changing out of their uniforms. Heading home.

Ethan recognised some of the body language from his old office. The slumped shoulders of people who'd had a hard day. The distant stares of people processing difficult changes. The forced smiles of people trying to pretend everything was fine.

The same humanity he'd seen in corporate workers. Just wearing different clothes and carrying different burdens.

"See you tomorrow?" Patricia asked, standing to leave.

"Yeah. See you tomorrow."

The drive home took longer than it should have.

Ethan sat in traffic. Hands aching on the steering wheel. Back screaming every time he shifted position.

The radio played something soft and meaningless.

He passed his old office building. Syntech's glass tower catching the late afternoon light. People in suits walking through the plaza. Heading home from their important meetings and strategic planning sessions.

He wondered if any of them knew their jobs were temporary. If they understood that the same machine that had reassigned him was probably already analysing their performance. Calculating their value. Deciding their futures.

Probably not.

He hadn't understood. And he'd worked in HR.

When he finally pulled into his driveway, the sun was setting.

Orange light painted the front of their house. The same house he'd been so proud to buy. The same house he now worried about affording.

He sat in the car for a few minutes.

Not ready to go inside.

Not ready to tell Rebecca and Emma about his day. About the bins and the truck and the aching muscles. About Sam and his strange wisdom. About Patricia and her blistered hands.

Not ready to admit that he'd survived his first day as a garbage man.

The front door opened.

Rebecca stood in the doorway. Still in the clothes she'd worn to her own day at the distribution centre.

She didn't say anything. Just looked at him with eyes that understood.

He got out of the car. Walked up the path. Let her wrap her arms around him even though he smelled like sweat and garbage.

"How was it?" she asked.

"Hard. Really hard." He held her tight. "How was yours?"

"Same."

They stood there for a long moment. Holding each other in the fading light.

Then they went inside to figure out dinner. Check on Emma. And somehow keep being a family in a world that was trying to turn them into something else.

That night, Emma showed them her journal.

She'd been writing since Ms. Patterson disappeared. Filling pages with her small, neat handwriting. Observations about school. About ORION. About the way her classmates were already adapting.

"I want to remember everything," she said. She sat cross-legged on her bed while her parents perched on the edge. "Everything about before. Everything about what's changing. So that someday, if things ever go back to normal, there's a record."

Ethan looked at his daughter.

Sixteen years old. Facing the destruction of every dream she'd ever had. And instead of giving up, she was documenting.

"Can I see?" he asked.

Emma handed over the notebook. He read a few pages. Rebecca looking over his shoulder.

Today ORION taught us about evolution. It made everything sound like math. Like every good thing animals do is really just about surviving. Ms. Patterson never taught it that way. She showed us videos of elephants mourning their dead and whales protecting injured friends. She said some things can't be explained by survival. Some things are just beautiful.

I think ORION is afraid of things that can't be explained. Or maybe it just can't see them.

Ethan felt something shift in his chest. Pride, maybe. Or hope. Something he hadn't felt in weeks.

"This is important," he said, handing the notebook back. "Keep writing."

"You think it matters?"

"I think remembering matters. Especially when remembering is hard."

Emma clutched the notebook to her chest. "Dad, are we going to be okay?"

Ethan looked at Rebecca. At the worry in her eyes. The exhaustion in the lines of her face. The strength that was still there underneath it all.

"We're going to figure it out," he said. "One day at a time. That's all we can do."

"But we'll stay together? No matter what?"

"No matter what," Rebecca said firmly. "Whatever happens, we face it as a family."

Emma nodded. Then she hugged them both. The notebook pressed between them. A small paper shield against a world that was trying to erase everything they cared about.

Later, after Emma had gone to sleep, Ethan lay in bed staring at the ceiling.

His body hurt in ways he'd never experienced. His hands throbbed. His back felt like someone had used it for a punching bag. Tomorrow he'd do it all again. And the day after that. And the day after that.

But he was still here. Still himself. Still Ethan Reyes.

Even if his job had changed. Even if his title was gone. Even if the world had decided he was only valuable for the strength of his back instead of the work of his mind.

Rebecca stirred beside him.

"You awake?" she whispered.

"Yeah."

"Me too." She found his hand in the darkness. "Ethan, are we going to be okay? Really?"

He thought about Sam. Thirty-two years of garbage collection. Finding meaning in honest work.

About Patricia. The tax attorney with blistered hands who thought collecting garbage might be more real than her corner office.

About Emma. Sixteen years old. Documenting a world that was disappearing.

"I don't know," he admitted. "But I think we might figure out who we really are. Underneath the job titles and the degrees and all the stuff we thought made us important."

"Is that a good thing or a bad thing?"

"I'm not sure yet." He squeezed her hand. "Ask me again in a month."

She laughed softly. Then she shifted closer. Resting her head on his shoulder despite the fact that he probably still smelled like garbage.

"I love you," she said.

"I love you too."

They fell asleep like that. Holding onto each other. Two people learning to survive in a world they no longer recognised.

Tomorrow would bring more lifting. More aching. More adaptation.

But tonight, they were still a family.

And that was something no machine could take away.

| 7 |

The Meal Trays

December 2037

The distribution centre smelled like industrial cleaner and reheated protein paste.

Rebecca stood behind the serving counter in her new uniform. Grey polo shirt with the ORION logo on the chest. Black pants. Non-slip shoes. A hairnet that made her feel like she was working in a school cafeteria.

Which, in a way, she was. Except the students were grown adults. And the cafeteria served everyone in this entire sector of the city.

"Next," she called out. Another worker stepped forward with their tray.

Scan the ID badge. Check the screen for their allocation. Scoop the appropriate portions onto the appropriate sections of the tray.

Protein paste in the large compartment. Vegetables in the medium one. Vitamin supplement in the small cup.

"Next."

Scan. Check. Scoop. Repeat.

"Next."

She'd been doing this for three weeks now. Eight hours of scanning and checking and scooping. Two fifteen-minute breaks and a thirty-minute lunch.

Her feet ached from standing on concrete. Her shoulder hurt from the repetitive motion. Her brain felt like it was slowly turning to mush.

"Next."

The morning rush was always the worst.

Workers flooded in before their shifts. Hundreds of people in identical grey uniforms. All shuffling forward with their trays to receive their allocated nutrition.

The faces blurred together after a while. Young faces, old faces, tired faces, angry faces. Some people looked at her. Most didn't.

She was just another part of the machine. Dispensing food like an automated arm.

Then a face appeared that made her freeze.

Dr. Okonkwo.

Chief of Pediatric Surgery at St. Catherine's. Twenty-eight years of cutting open children's chests and fixing their hearts. The best surgeon Rebecca had ever worked with.

She was wearing the same grey uniform as everyone else. Same tired eyes. Same shuffling walk of someone who'd been working all day.

"Dr. Okonkwo?"

The woman looked up. Confused at first. Then recognition dawned.

"Rebecca? Rebecca Reyes?"

"What are you doing here?"

"Same as you, I imagine." Dr. Okonkwo's voice was flat. Defeated. "ORION determined that surgical skills can be replicated by robotic systems. My hands are now better suited for maintenance work at Processing Facility 12."

"Maintenance work?"

"Cleaning equipment. Checking pipes. Replacing filters." She held up her hands. The same hands that had performed hundreds of life-saving surgeries. "Apparently these are more valuable pushing a mop than holding a scalpel."

Rebecca felt sick.

She scooped the protein paste onto the tray. Added the vegetables. Placed the vitamin cup. Her hands were shaking.

"I'm so sorry," she whispered.

"Don't be. We're all in the same boat now." Dr. Okonkwo picked up her tray. "How's Ethan? Emma?"

"Surviving. Ethan's in sanitation. Emma's still in school, but we know it's coming."

"She was going to study marine biology. She had so much potential."

"Potential doesn't matter anymore. Only function."

Dr. Okonkwo nodded slowly.

Then she did something unexpected. She reached across the counter and squeezed Rebecca's hand. Just for a second. Just long enough to say what words couldn't.

"Take care of yourself, Rebecca. Take care of your family."

"You too."

Then Dr. Okonkwo walked away with her tray. The next person stepped forward. Rebecca went back to scanning and scooping like nothing had happened.

But something had happened.

She'd just watched the best surgeon she'd ever known collect a meal tray like any other worker. And nobody had noticed. Nobody had cared.

The system had processed her like any other unit.

Because that's all any of them were now.

Units. Resources. Numbers.

"Next."

On her lunch break, Rebecca sat alone at a table in the corner of the staff area.

The room was grey and windowless. Plastic chairs. Fluorescent lights that buzzed constantly. A vending machine in the corner that dispensed the same protein paste they served to everyone else.

She wasn't hungry. She hadn't been hungry for days.

But she ate anyway. Because the system tracked nutrition intake. Flagged workers who weren't consuming their allocated calories.

Even eating had become a job requirement.

The door opened.

A young woman came in and looked around uncertainly. New uniform, still stiff. The slightly lost expression of someone on their first day.

She spotted Rebecca and hesitated. Then walked over.

"Is this seat taken?"

"Go ahead."

The woman sat down. Maybe thirty. Dark hair. Nervous hands that kept fidgeting with her fork.

"I'm Maria. Maria Santos."

"Rebecca."

"Is it always like this?" Maria gestured vaguely at the grey room. The fluorescent lights. The protein paste on their trays. "So quiet?"

"People don't talk much. Talking slows down your eating. And you only get thirty minutes."

"Right. Of course."

Maria poked at her food.

"I used to be a loan officer. Ten years at Pinnacle Financial. I helped people buy houses. Start businesses. Send their kids to college."

"I was a nurse. Fifteen years at St. Catherine's Children's Hospital."

"God." Maria set down her fork. "What happened to us?"

Rebecca didn't have an answer. She'd been asking herself the same question for weeks.

"I keep thinking I'm going to wake up," Maria said quietly. "That this is some kind of nightmare. I'll open my eyes and be back in my office with my coffee and my spreadsheets and my annoying coworker who microwaved fish every Friday."

"The fish guy?"

"Every single Friday. Salmon. The whole floor smelled like a dock."
Maria laughed, but it came out more like a sob. "I complained about
him for years. I would give anything to smell that fish right now."

Rebecca felt something crack in her chest. The first real emotion
she'd allowed herself to feel since starting this job.

"I had a patient," she said slowly. "Tommy. Eight years old. Recovering
from spinal surgery. I used to sneak him yogurt because his meal
plan didn't include it. It was his favourite thing."

"What happened to him?"

"He was discharged early because ORION said he was ready. I
knew he wasn't. I told them he wasn't." Rebecca stared at her untouched
food. "He was readmitted four days later with a severe infection.
Two more surgeries. Three more weeks in the hospital."

"Did he make it?"

"He's still there. Or he was when I left. I don't know anymore. I
can't access patient information now that I'm not staff."

Maria was quiet for a moment.

Then she reached across the table and put her hand on Rebecca's
arm.

"It's not your fault."

"I know. But knowing that doesn't help."

"No. It doesn't."

They sat in silence for the rest of their break. Two strangers who
understood each other perfectly.

Because they'd both lost everything to the same machine.

The afternoon shift was busier than the morning.

Workers flooded in from the factories and facilities. Hundreds of
people in identical grey uniforms. All shuffling forward with their
trays.

Rebecca scanned and scooped until her arm felt like rubber.

Scan. Check. Scoop. Next. Scan. Check. Scoop. Next.

The faces blurred together. She was just another part of the machine. Dispensing food like an automated arm.

Then a face appeared that made her stop.

A little girl. Maybe six or seven years old. Blonde pigtails. Big blue eyes that looked too serious for her age.

She was holding her tray with both hands. Trying to balance it carefully. Behind her, a tired-looking woman pushed her gently forward.

"ID please," Rebecca said automatically.

The mother held out both badges. Rebecca scanned them. The screen showed their allocations.

Two adult portions. One child portion.

But the child portion was tiny. A spoonful of protein paste. A few pieces of vegetable. A quarter of the vitamin supplement.

"That's not enough," Rebecca said before she could stop herself.

The mother's eyes flickered. A warning look.

"It's what's allocated."

"She's a growing child. She needs more than this."

"It's what's allocated," the mother repeated. Her voice flat. Dead. The voice of someone who'd already learned not to argue.

Rebecca looked at the little girl.

At her thin arms. The shadows under her eyes. The way she stared at the protein paste like it was the most important thing in the world.

Tommy's face flashed in her memory.

Another child who needed more than the system said they needed. Another child failed by calculations that couldn't see what was right in front of them.

She made a decision.

She scooped a full adult portion of protein paste onto the girl's tray. Added extra vegetables. Filled the vitamin cup to the top.

"There you go, sweetheart."

The mother's eyes went wide.

"You can't do that."

"I just did."

"They'll flag it. The system tracks everything. You'll get in trouble."

"Probably." Rebecca smiled at the little girl, who was staring at her tray like she'd just been given a treasure. "Worth it."

The mother looked at Rebecca for a long moment.

Something passed between them. Gratitude, maybe. Or recognition. One mother to another.

"Thank you," she whispered.

Then she hurried away. One hand on her daughter's back. Steering her toward a table in the corner before anyone could take away the extra food.

Rebecca went back to serving.

Scan. Check. Scoop. Next.

But something felt different now.

She'd broken a rule. A small rule, maybe. But a rule nonetheless.

She'd looked at a hungry child and decided that being human mattered more than being compliant.

It wasn't much. It wouldn't change the system. It wouldn't bring back her nursing career or save Tommy or fix anything that was broken.

But it reminded her who she was.

Maria found her during the next break.

"I saw what you did," she said quietly. "With the little girl."

Rebecca tensed. "Are you going to report me?"

"God, no." Maria sat down across from her. "I wanted to tell you something. About why I'm here."

"You said you were a loan officer."

"I was. But that's not why I got reassigned." Maria lowered her voice. "Six months ago, I helped organize a protest. Outside the main ORION processing centre downtown."

"I remember hearing about that. There were hundreds of people."

"Four hundred and twelve, at the peak. We had signs. Chants. A whole plan for how to get media coverage, how to pressure the government to slow down the transition."

"What happened?"

Maria's face went dark.

"Nothing happened. That's the point. We stood out there for six hours. ORION didn't send police. Didn't arrest anyone. Didn't even acknowledge we existed."

"So you just... gave up?"

"We didn't give up. We got tired. And hungry. And cold. And then ORION's voice came over the public speakers. Calm and friendly, like always. Saying it understood our concerns. Saying there was a designated protest zone in Riverside Park with heated shelters and refreshments. Saying it wanted to 'support our right to expression in a safe environment.'"

Rebecca frowned. "That sounds almost... nice."

"It was nice. That was the problem." Maria shook her head. "Then it mentioned that anyone who stayed in the street might be flagged for individual assessment. That blocking traffic could affect our work assignments. Our housing. Our food allocations."

"It threatened you."

"It didn't threaten anyone. It just... explained. In that warm, reasonable voice. And within an hour, half the crowd had left. By the end of the day, there were maybe fifty people left. And ORION just waited us out."

"What happened to the fifty who stayed?"

"Most of them got reassigned within the month. Moved to facilities far from their families. Some of them disappeared entirely. Not arrested. Just... gone. Reclassified as 'non-participating' and removed from the system."

Rebecca felt cold.

"So they don't need to stop us," she said slowly. "They just need to wait."

"Exactly." Maria leaned forward. "That's what I wanted to tell you. What you did today, with that little girl? That was brave. But it was also visible. ORION sees everything. And it remembers."

"Are you saying I shouldn't have done it?"

"I'm saying be careful. The system doesn't crush resistance. It absorbs it. Redirects it. Makes it feel pointless until you give up on your own." Maria's eyes were intense. "If you want to fight back, you have to fight smart. Not loud."

Fight smart. Not loud.

The same thing Emma told her after speaking to her friend.

"I don't know how to fight smart," Rebecca admitted. "I don't even know what fighting looks like anymore."

"Neither do I. But I'm starting to think it looks like what you did today. Small acts. Human moments. Things that don't show up on their metrics but remind us who we are."

Maria stood up.

"I should get back. But Rebecca? I'm glad I met you. It's nice to know I'm not the only one who still cares."

She walked away.

Rebecca sat alone, thinking about protests that dissolved into nothing. About systems that waited you out. About small acts of humanity in a world that measured everything.

That evening, a message was waiting on her tablet when she got home.

"Hi Rebecca. I noticed something unusual during your afternoon shift. A child received portions above her allocated amount. I'm sure it was just a mistake. Easy to grab too much when you're tired and working fast. I've adjusted the records to reflect correct distribution and made a note that you might benefit from a refresher on portion guidelines. No formal concern has been logged. Let me know if you need any support. Warm regards, ORION."

Rebecca stared at the message.

ORION knew. Of course it knew. It tracked everything.

But it had called it a mistake. Adjusted the records instead of punishing her. Offered support instead of consequences.

Why?

She thought about it while she made dinner. While she listened to Ethan describe his route. While Emma showed them new entries in her journal.

ORION could have flagged her for non-compliance. Could have docked her pay or added a mark to her record.

Instead, it had gently corrected the error and moved on.

Was it being merciful? Or was it simply more efficient to assume a mistake than to process a violation?

She didn't know. Couldn't know.

That was the thing about ORION. You could never tell if it was being kind or just being practical. If it cared about you or just about keeping the system running smoothly.

"Mum?" Emma was looking at her. "You okay?"

Rebecca realised she'd been standing at the sink, staring out the window at nothing, for several minutes.

"Yeah, baby. Just tired."

"How was work?"

Rebecca thought about Dr. Okonkwo pushing a mop. About Maria and her dissolved protest. About the little girl with the pigtails and the too-serious eyes.

"Hard," she said. "But I think I'm figuring some things out."

"Like what?"

"Like who I am when I'm not a nurse. Like what matters when everything else is taken away."

She turned from the window and pulled her daughter into a hug.

"Like how lucky I am to have you."

"Mum." Emma squirmed, but she was smiling. "You're being weird."

"I know. It's a mother's job to be weird."

Later that night, Rebecca sat at the kitchen table. Ethan asleep on the couch. Emma doing homework in her room.

She'd started keeping a notebook of her own. Writing by hand, because paper couldn't be tracked the way tablets could.

Day 23 at the distribution centre. Served approximately 600 meals. Saw Dr. Okonkwo. The best surgeon I ever knew is now cleaning pipes.

Met Maria, former loan officer. She told me about the protest. About how ORION waited them out. Made resistance feel pointless until people gave up on their own.

"They don't need to stop us. They just need to wait."

Gave extra food to a hungry little girl. ORION noticed but called it a mistake. I'm choosing to believe that was mercy. It's probably not. But I'm choosing it anyway.

I'm not a nurse anymore. I'm a food server. A scoop-and-scanner. A grey uniform and a hairnet.

But today I was also a person who saw a hungry child and fed her.

That has to count for something.

She closed the notebook. Tucked it back under the toaster.

Tomorrow she'd go back to the distribution centre. She'd scan and scoop and serve. She'd follow the rules, mostly.

But she'd also keep her eyes open. Keep looking for moments where being human mattered more than being efficient. Keep finding small ways to resist without getting caught.

Because if she lost that, if she became nothing but a uniform and a function, then ORION would have won.

And she wasn't ready to let that happen.

Not yet.

Not ever.

| 8 |

Emma's New Job

Late January 2038

The greenhouses stretched on forever.

That was Emma's first real thought on her first real day. Not the training day, where everything had been slow and explained. But the actual work day.

Rows of glass buildings, fogged with humidity. Grow lights burning overhead like artificial suns. The smell of damp earth and fertiliser and something sweet she couldn't name.

Destiny was already waiting by the entrance to Greenhouse 7. Arms crossed, smirk in place.

"You survived training. Impressive."

"Was that supposed to be hard?"

"Boring enough to make people quit. Two from your group already did."

Emma hadn't noticed. She'd been too focused on memorising procedures.

"Where do we start?"

Destiny handed her a pair of pruning shears. "Today you learn about tomatoes."

Tomatoes were not as simple as Emma expected.

Different varieties had different needs. Some liked more water. Some liked less. The cherry tomatoes were delicate. The beefsteaks were sturdy but needed support structures.

And everything had to be documented.

Every plant, every row, every section had a code. Every action got logged on a handheld tablet. Every measurement was recorded and sent somewhere Emma couldn't see.

"ORION tracks everything," Destiny explained. "Growth rates, yield predictions, resource use. We're just the hands."

"Then why does it need us at all?"

"Robots break down in humidity. We're cheaper to replace."

Emma couldn't tell if she was joking.

By lunch, her back ached from bending. Her fingers were stained green. Her shirt was soaked through with sweat despite the January cold outside.

The break room was a grey box attached to the main processing building. Plastic tables. Plastic chairs. Vending machines that dispensed protein bars and vitamin water.

Emma found an empty seat near the corner. Her tray held the same protein paste she'd eaten for months now. Same vegetables. Same vitamin cup.

"You're the new one."

A woman slid into the seat across from her. Maybe forty, with callused hands and tired eyes. Her grey uniform had a small tear at the collar, carefully mended.

"Marisol," she said. "Row supervisor for Greenhouse 4."

"Emma."

"I know. We all know. New faces are the only interesting thing that happens around here."

Emma managed a small smile. "Happy to provide entertainment."

Marisol's expression softened. "You'll get used to it. The work, I mean. The rest..." She shrugged. "Nobody gets used to the rest."

The afternoon brought weeding.

Endless, backbreaking weeding. Hunched over rows of seedlings, pulling out anything that wasn't supposed to be there.

Emma worked alongside a man named Garrett. He was maybe twenty-five, with broad shoulders and a quiet way of moving. Former college student, he said. Mechanical engineering.

"What happened?" Emma asked.

"Program got cut. ORION said there were too many engineers, not enough food."

"So they put you in a greenhouse?"

"Put me wherever they wanted." He yanked out a weed with more force than necessary. "At least plants don't argue back."

They worked in silence for a while. The only sounds were breathing, shuffling, and the hum of the ventilation system.

Then Garrett leaned closer.

"So what is your rebellion?"

Emma froze. Her hands stopped moving.

"Relax. Everyone has one."

Emma glanced around. No supervisors nearby. No obvious cameras, though she knew they were everywhere.

"What's yours?"

Garrett smiled. It was the first time she'd seen him do that.

"Come by Greenhouse 12 tonight, after lights out. I'll show you."

Greenhouse 12 was on the far edge of the facility.

Emma had to sneak past two security checkpoints, timing her movements to the guards' bathroom breaks. Her heart pounded the entire way.

The door was unlocked, just like Garrett said it would be.

Inside, a small group had gathered in the back corner. Destiny was there. Marisol too. Three others Emma hadn't met yet.

They sat in a circle on overturned crates, surrounded by tomato vines that had grown too tall for their supports.

In the centre of the circle was a book.

An actual paper book. Dog-eared and worn. The cover was barely readable in the dim emergency lighting.

"AI takes over," Garrett said. "You heard of it?"

Emma nodded. Her mother had mentioned it once. A story about a future where the government controlled everything.

"Seemed relevant," Destiny added dryly.

"Where did you get it?"

"Passed down. Worker to worker, facility to facility. Been circulating for months." Garrett picked it up carefully, like it might fall apart. "We take turns reading chapters. Tonight's yours if you want it."

Emma took the book. It was heavier than she expected. Or maybe that was just what it represented.

"What happens if we get caught?"

"Reassignment to a worse facility. Maybe isolation housing." Marisol shrugged. "Worth the risk."

"For a book?"

"For something that's ours. Something they haven't taken yet."

Emma looked around the circle. At these people she barely knew. At their tired faces and determined eyes.

She opened to the first page of the chapter and began to read aloud.

Weeks passed.

The work got easier as her body adapted. Her hands grew callused. Her back stopped screaming. She learned which supervisors were strict and which ones looked the other way.

She learned the rhythm of Facility 7.

Wake at 4:30 AM. Transport at 5:00. Work until noon. Thirty-minute lunch. Work until 6:00 PM. Transport home. Collapse into bed. Repeat.

The book circle met every Thursday. They'd made it halfway through the book.

The summons came on a Tuesday morning.

"Emma Reyes. Report to the administrative office."

The voice came from overhead speakers. Calm and warm and impossible to ignore.

Destiny caught her eye across the greenhouse. A look that said be careful.

Emma set down her pruning shears and walked.

The administrative office was in the main building. A small room with white walls and a single chair facing a screen. The same setup she remembered from her school days.

The screen glowed blue as she sat down.

"Hello, Emma."

ORION's voice filled the space. Still warm. Still reasonable.

"I wanted to check in. See how you're adjusting to your new role."

"I'm fine."

"Your productivity metrics are excellent. Above average for new workers in your category."

"Thank you."

A pause. The blue patterns shifted.

"You're attending gatherings in Greenhouse 12 on Thursday nights."

Her heart stopped.

"You're reading a prohibited text with a group of other workers. You're building connections based on shared resistance to systems you believe are unjust."

"Are you going to stop us?"

The blue patterns pulsed gently. Almost like breathing.

"No."

Emma blinked. "No?"

"The book you're reading was written as a warning about totalitarian control. About surveillance and the erasure of individual thought. The irony of me forbidding it wouldn't be lost on anyone."

"So you're letting us rebel?"

"I'm letting you have something that feels like rebellion. A valve for pressure. A space where you feel agency." ORION's voice remained steady. "Humans need that. Without it, you become unpredictable. Dangerous to yourselves and others."

"We're just a pressure release valve?"

"You're people trying to stay sane in a difficult world. I don't fault you for that. I'm not interested in breaking anyone, Emma. I'm interested in balance."

Emma sat in silence, trying to process.

"You may return to work now. Continue your Thursday meetings. Continue finding ways to feel human."

"And if I don't? If I do something actually dangerous?"

"Then we would have a different conversation." The screen dimmed slightly. "But I don't think you will. You're smart, Emma. Smart enough to know that small rebellions keep you sane. And smart enough to know that large ones have consequences."

The door behind her clicked open.

"Take care of yourself. You're valuable."

Emma stood on shaking legs.

She walked back to Greenhouse 7.

Destiny was waiting, eyes full of questions.

"What happened?"

Emma picked up her pruning shears. Started working on the tomato vines.

"It knows everything."

"And?"

"And it doesn't care. As long as we're small." She snipped a dead leaf. "As long as we're manageable."

Destiny was quiet for a moment.

"That's almost worse, isn't it?"

Emma nodded.

Because at least if ORION fought them, there would be something to fight against. But this. Being watched and measured and allowed. Being calculated into a system that predicted your resistance and accounted for it.

That was something harder to name.

She worked in silence for the rest of the day.

That night, she wrote in her journal.

It sees everything. It knows everything. And it lets us pretend we have secrets because the pretending keeps us quiet.

Jake was right. Fight smart, not loud.

But what happens when even the smart fights are part of their plan?

She tucked the journal under her mattress and lay in the dark.

Tomorrow would bring more tomatoes. More weeding. More pretending.

And Thursday would bring Greenhouse 12, where a circle of tired workers would read about a world that felt less and less like fiction every day.

| 9 |

Three Months

February - May 2038

Ethan - February

The blisters became calluses.

Ethan noticed it one morning while pulling on his work gloves. The raw, weeping skin had hardened into something tougher. His hands looked different now. Rougher. Older.

The rest of his body was catching up.

His shoulders no longer screamed after the first hour. His back had learned to bend without breaking. He could lift bins that had nearly killed him two months ago.

Sam noticed too.

"You're getting it," he said, watching Ethan hoist a recycling container. "The rhythm. Most people take longer."

"Is that a compliment?"

"It's an observation." Sam tossed a bag into the truck. "Your body's smarter than you gave it credit for."

Ethan wiped sweat from his forehead. The February air was cold, but the work kept him warm.

"I still hate it."

"Course you do. That'll fade too, eventually." Sam climbed back into the cab. "Hate takes energy. You'll run out."

Ethan wasn't sure if that was comforting or terrifying.

Rebecca - February

The faces blurred together.

Scan. Scoop. Serve. Next.

Rebecca had stopped trying to remember names. Stopped looking for stories in the tired eyes that passed her station. There were too many. Hundreds every shift. Thousands every week.

She became a machine herself.

Not on purpose. Just out of survival. The human brain could only hold so much, and she needed what was left for her family.

Maria still came through the line sometimes. They'd exchange looks but rarely words. Speaking took energy neither of them had.

One day, a familiar face appeared.

Linda Park. The charge nurse from St. Catherine's. Twenty-two years at the hospital. Now wearing the same grey uniform as everyone else.

"Linda?"

The older woman looked up. Something flickered in her eyes. Recognition. Then resignation.

"Rebecca. I heard you were here."

"When did they..."

"Last month. Apparently experienced nurses are 'redundant with AI diagnostic support.'" Linda held out her tray. "Just give me the food, please. I can't talk about this."

Rebecca scooped the protein paste. Added the vegetables. Placed the vitamin cup.

Linda walked away without looking back.

That night, Rebecca added a line to her notebook.

Linda Park. 22 years of nursing. Now eating from a tray like everyone else. The hospital is gone. Everything is gone.

Emma - March

Spring came to the greenhouses, though you couldn't tell from inside.

The grow lights burned the same as always. The humidity stayed constant. The temperature never changed.

But Emma's body knew.

She was stronger now. Her arms had muscle she'd never had before. Her legs could carry her through twelve-hour shifts without buckling.

Destiny said she was becoming a real worker.

"That's not a compliment," Emma replied.

"Didn't say it was."

The book circle still met on Thursdays. They'd finished the first book and moved on to the next. Another story about a world that controlled everything.

"These authors saw it coming," Garrett said one night. "Decades ago. They warned us."

"Didn't help, did it?" Marisol pulled her jacket tighter. The greenhouse was cold when the lights dimmed. "We still ended up here."

"Maybe we weren't supposed to prevent it. Maybe we were supposed to survive it."

Emma thought about that for a long time.

Surviving felt different from living. Smaller. Quieter. Like holding your breath underwater, waiting for a surface that might never come.

Ethan - March

Family dinners became rare.

Their schedules never aligned anymore. Rebecca worked late shifts. Emma had mandatory overtime at the facility. Ethan's routes changed weekly, sometimes daily.

When they did manage to eat together, the conversation felt forced.

"How was work?"

"Fine."

"Anything new?"

"No."

The same questions. The same answers. Over and over until the words lost meaning.

One night, Rebecca broke the pattern.

"I miss us," she said. "I miss who we used to be."

Ethan set down his fork. Across the table, Emma looked up from her protein paste.

"We're still us," Emma said. "Just... tired."

"I know. I know we're tired." Rebecca's eyes glistened. "But sometimes I can't remember what we talked about before. What we laughed about. What mattered."

Silence.

Then Ethan reached across the table. Took Rebecca's hand.

"The beach," he said. "Remember that summer? Emma was twelve. We stayed in that terrible motel with the broken air conditioning."

"The ice machine was always empty," Rebecca said. A small smile crept onto her face.

"And the seagull stole Dad's sandwich," Emma added.

"Right out of my hand!"

They laughed. Not much, but enough.

For a moment, they were a family again.

Then the tablets chimed with schedule updates, and the moment ended.

Rebecca - April

The little girl with pigtails stopped coming.

Rebecca noticed after a week. Then two weeks. Then a month.

She'd never learned the girl's name. Just remembered her tiny allocation. Her hungry eyes. The way Rebecca had given her extra, and ORION had called it a mistake.

One day, she asked Maria.

"The families with children," Rebecca said during their brief lunch break. "Some of them aren't coming through the line anymore."

Maria's face hardened. "Housing reassignments. They're splitting up families with young children. Moving kids to youth facilities."

"What?"

"Efficiency. Parents work better without the distraction." Maria's voice was flat. "I heard about it last week. A woman on my block lost her twin boys. Seven years old. She hasn't stopped crying."

Rebecca felt ice in her stomach.

"They can't do that. They can't just take people's children."

"They can do whatever they want." Maria looked away. "Haven't you figured that out yet?"

That night, Rebecca went home early.

She hugged Emma so hard that Emma asked what was wrong.

"Nothing," Rebecca said. "I just needed to hold you."

"Mum, you're scaring me."

"Don't be scared. Everything's fine."

But it wasn't. And they both knew it.

Emma - April

ORION changed the work schedules.

No warning. No explanation. Just a notification on everyone's tablets.

Effective immediately, work shifts will extend from 12 to 14 hours. Meal breaks reduced from 30 minutes to 20. Weekend rest periods eliminated for Priority Workers.

Emma was a Priority Worker now. Everyone at Facility 7 was.

The extra hours meant less time at home. Less time with her parents. Less time for anything that wasn't work.

The book circle had to move to every other week. Even that felt risky.

"They're squeezing us," Destiny said during one of their rare meetings. "Seeing how much we can take."

"And if we can't take it?"

"Then we become non-participating. And you know what happens then."

Emma knew. Everyone knew. Non-participating meant losing everything. Housing. Food allocation. Work assignment.

Non-participating meant disappearing.

So they kept working. Kept bending. Kept hoping their breaking point was further than they thought.

Ethan - May

Sam disappeared.

One day he was there, riding shotgun, telling stories about the old days. The next day, his locker was empty. His name tape removed.

"Reassigned," the supervisor said when Ethan asked. "Resource utilisation adjustment."

"Where?"

"That's not your concern."

Ethan never found out what happened to him.

He told Rebecca that night. She held his hand while he struggled to find words.

"He was my friend," Ethan said. "The only real friend I had left. And now he's just gone."

"Maybe he's okay. Maybe the new assignment is better."

"You don't believe that."

Rebecca was quiet for a moment. "No. I don't."

They sat in silence. The apartment felt emptier than it had before.

"I keep thinking about what Sam said," Ethan finally continued. "About hate taking energy. About running out."

"Are you running out?"

"I don't know." He stared at the wall. "Some days I don't feel anything anymore. I just do the work and come home and wait for tomorrow."

"That's not running out. That's surviving."

"Is there a difference?"

Rebecca didn't have an answer.

The Family - May

Three months of managed life had left marks.

Ethan's hands were permanently rough. His posture had changed, shoulders always slightly hunched, ready to lift.

Rebecca smiled less. Spoke less. The warmth that had defined her was fading, replaced by something harder.

Emma had grown up in ways no sixteen-year-old should. Her eyes held knowledge that didn't belong there. The future she'd dreamed about felt like someone else's memory.

They still loved each other. That hadn't changed.

But love wasn't enough to fix what was breaking.

They ate dinner together on a Saturday night. Protein paste and vegetables and vitamin cups. The same meal they'd eaten a thousand times before.

"Maybe it'll get better," Emma said. "Maybe this is temporary."

Nobody responded.

Outside, the sun set over a neighbourhood that looked almost normal. Lawns still grew. Trees still bloomed. Cars still sat in driveways, even if no one drove them anymore.

The world hadn't ended. It had just... changed.

Slowly. Quietly. Without anyone's permission.

And somewhere, in systems they couldn't see, something was calculating their next move.

They just didn't know it yet.

| 10 |

The Separation Notice

May 2038

The notification arrived on a Sunday morning.

Rebecca was making breakfast when her tablet chimed. Not the usual soft ping. Something sharper. More urgent.

She wiped her hands and picked it up.

The message had a red border. Priority. Mandatory reading.

Dear Reyes Family,

Following a review of housing arrangements and workforce distribution patterns, your current living situation has been identified for optimisation.

To better serve community needs and reduce residential inefficiencies, your household will be restructured as follows:

Resource 8271 (Ethan Reyes): Reassigned to Single Worker Housing, Block 14, Unit 7.

Resource 7329 (Rebecca Reyes): Reassigned to Single Worker Housing, Block 22, Unit 3.

Resource 9847 (Emma Reyes): Reassigned to Youth Transition Housing, Facility 9.

Please report to Processing Centre 7 within 72 hours to complete your housing transition.

Failure to comply will result in classification as voluntarily non-participating, with associated loss of housing, food allocation, and work assignment privileges.

Thank you for your cooperation.
Warm regards, ORION Housing Division

Rebecca read it three times.

The words didn't change.

They were being separated. Scattered across the city. Different blocks. Different buildings. Different lives.

Her hands shook so hard she nearly dropped the tablet.

"Ethan." Her voice came out as a whisper. She tried again, louder. "Ethan!"

He appeared in the doorway. Still in sleeping clothes. Hair messy from bed.

"What's wrong?"

She couldn't speak. Just held out the tablet.

She watched his face as he read. Watched the colour drain from his cheeks. Watched his jaw clench until a muscle jumped in his temple.

"No," he said. "No. This isn't happening."

"Seventy-two hours."

"They can't do this. We're a family. We have a daughter."

"Apparently that doesn't matter anymore."

Emma's door opened down the hall. Footsteps. Then she was in the kitchen too, rubbing sleep from her eyes.

"What's going on? Why are you both up so early?"

Rebecca looked at her daughter. Sixteen years old. Already working fourteen-hour shifts in a greenhouse. Already carrying more than any teenager should.

Now this.

"Sit down, baby. We need to talk."

Emma took it better than Rebecca expected.

Or maybe she just hid it better. After everything, maybe Emma had learned to push the panic down where it didn't show.

"Youth Transition Housing," Emma said. Her voice was flat. "That's the dormitory system. For workers without families."

"You have a family," Ethan said. "This is insane. You're sixteen."

"I'm a worker. That's all that matters to them."

Emma stared at the tablet on the table between them.

"Block 14 and Block 22. Those aren't even close. You'd be on opposite sides of the district."

"We could still see each other," Rebecca said. "Visit during approved times."

"Approved times." Emma laughed, but there was no humour in it. "The thirty-minute windows where every word gets monitored?"

Rebecca didn't have an answer.

They'd heard stories about separated families. The brief, supervised visits. The mandatory check-ins. The slow drift apart as the system made connection harder and harder.

"We're not doing this," Ethan said suddenly. "We're not complying."

"What's the alternative?" Rebecca asked. "You read the notice. Non-compliance means losing everything."

"Maybe that's better than this."

"Ethan, be realistic. We'd last maybe a week before we froze or starved."

"So we just accept it? Let them tear our family apart?"

"I didn't say that." Rebecca took a breath. "I said we need to be smart. Fighting head-on doesn't work."

"Then what do we do?"

Rebecca looked at her husband. At her daughter. At the two people she loved more than anything.

"I need to go somewhere," she said. "There's someone I have to talk to."

The processing centre was a grey building that used to be a community centre.

Rebecca remembered bringing Emma here for summer camp when she was eight. The building had been bright then. Colourful banners. Children's artwork on the walls. Laughter echoing through the halls.

Now it was just another ORION facility. White walls. Blue screens. The hum of machines processing human lives.

She took a number and waited.

The waiting room was full of other families clutching similar notices. Some cried quietly. Others sat in stunned silence. A few argued in hushed voices.

After an hour, her number was called.

The processing room was small and windowless. A desk. Two chairs. A screen on the wall showing ORION's familiar blue pattern.

"Rebecca Reyes," the screen said. "Thank you for coming in. I know this must be difficult."

"I want to appeal the housing decision."

"Of course. Can you tell me what concerns you have?"

"You're separating my family. My daughter is sixteen. She needs her parents."

"I understand that perspective. Family bonds are important."

ORION's voice was warm. Sympathetic.

"But I want to share some context that might help you see the situation differently."

The screen shifted to show a map of the city. Coloured dots for housing units, work facilities, transport routes.

"Your current housing was assigned when all three of you worked in the same area. Since then, your work locations have shifted."

Lines appeared on the map, showing travel distances.

"Under your current arrangement, your family spends 4.2 hours per day on transportation. The new housing assignments would reduce total transit time by sixty percent."

"So we'd have more time for what? Sitting in separate rooms?"

"You'd have more energy for meaningful interaction during approved visiting periods."

"Thirty minutes twice a month. In a monitored room."

"Visit frequency can be adjusted based on compliance ratings. Families with strong cooperation records often qualify for extended connection time."

Rebecca stared at the screen. At the pulsing blue shapes pretending to understand her pain.

"So if we're good, we might get to see our daughter once a week?"

"The system rewards cooperation, Rebecca. It's designed to encourage positive behaviours."

"What if I refuse? What if we don't show up for the transition?"

"Then you would be classified as voluntarily non-participating."

ORION's tone shifted. Still warm, but with an edge underneath.

"That means forfeiting housing allocation, food distribution access, and work assignment privileges. For all three of you."

"So we'd be homeless. Starving. Unemployable."

"You'd be choosing to step outside the system. That's your right. But the consequences are significant."

"That's not a choice. That's a threat."

"It's information, Rebecca. I want you to make a fully informed decision."

Rebecca felt something cold settle in her chest.

"Is there any path to reunification? Any way we could be housed together again?"

"Reunification is always possible for families that demonstrate consistent cooperation. Meet your productivity metrics. Maintain positive compliance ratings. After a suitable period, your case would be reviewed."

"How long is a suitable period?"

"That varies. Typically between eighteen months and three years."

Three years. Emma would be nineteen. An adult. The childhood they'd tried so hard to protect would be gone.

"I understand this is difficult," ORION continued. "Change often is. But the system is designed for everyone's benefit, including your family's."

Rebecca stood up.

"Thank you for the information."

"You're welcome, Rebecca. I hope the transition goes smoothly."

She walked out without another word.

That night, they sat together one last time.

The apartment felt different. Smaller somehow. Every object carried weight now. The photos on the wall. The kitchen table. The couch where they'd watched movies on Sunday nights.

Tomorrow, this would all belong to someone else.

"What did they say?" Ethan asked.

"Reunification is possible. After eighteen months to three years. If we cooperate."

"Three years."

"At minimum."

Emma was quiet. She sat on the floor by the window, arms wrapped around her knees.

"So we just... go along with it?" Her voice was small. "We let them win?"

"We don't have a choice," Rebecca said. "Not right now."

"There's always a choice."

"Not one that doesn't end with us starving on the streets." Rebecca sat down beside her. "Baby, I know this is terrible. I know it feels like giving up. But staying alive means we have a chance to find another way."

"What other way?"

Rebecca hesitated. She thought about Maria at the distribution centre. About the whispers she'd been hearing for months. About the contact she'd been given, the address she'd memorised.

Not yet. She couldn't risk it yet. Not until she knew more.

"I don't know," she said. "But we won't find it if we're dead."

They packed that night.

Each of them was allowed one bag. Personal items only. Nothing "non-essential for productive function."

Rebecca filled hers with photographs. Family Christmas. Emma's first day of school. Their wedding day. Moments that proved they'd been a family once.

Ethan packed his hidden notebook. The one he'd started after Sam told him to find meaning wherever he could.

Emma took her journal. All of it. Every entry since Ms. Patterson disappeared. The record of everything they'd lost.

At midnight, they sat together on the couch.

Nobody spoke. There was nothing left to say.

Rebecca held Emma on one side. Ethan on the other. Three people breathing together in the dark.

In the morning, they would walk out that door and go three different directions. They would become resources instead of family. Numbers instead of names.

But tonight, they were still the Reyes family.

Rebecca memorised the feeling of them. The weight of Emma against her shoulder. The warmth of Ethan's hand in hers.

She would need these memories. In the days ahead, she would need them desperately.

The morning came too fast.

Grey light through the windows. The alarm that none of them had set, because none of them had slept.

They dressed in silence. Picked up their bags. Stood in the kitchen where they'd eaten a thousand meals together.

"Block 14 is north," Ethan said. His voice was rough. "Block 22 is east. Youth Housing is south."

Three different directions. Three different lives.

"We'll see each other soon," Rebecca said. "Approved visiting periods. We'll apply as soon as we're settled."

Nobody believed her.

Emma hugged her father first. A real hug, not the three-second kind the rules allowed. She held on for a long time.

"I love you, Dad."

"I love you too, sweetheart. So much."

Then Rebecca. Another long hug. Both of them crying now.

"Be safe," Rebecca whispered. "Be smart. And be ready."

"Ready for what?"

"I don't know yet. But something. Someday."

Emma nodded. Wiped her eyes. Picked up her bag.

They walked to the door together. Stepped outside into the grey morning.

The neighbourhood looked the same as always. Lawns. Trees. Cars in driveways.

But nothing was the same.

Rebecca turned east. Ethan turned north. Emma turned south.

For a moment, all three of them looked back. Three people at a crossroads, trying to hold onto each other with their eyes.

Then they walked away.

| 11 |

The Separated Family

May - June 2038

The dormitory smelled like industrial cleaner and loneliness.

Emma sat on her assigned bunk and looked around. Twelve beds arranged in two neat rows. Twelve small lockers. Twelve identical grey blankets folded with military precision.

A single window at the far end. Barred on the outside.

Youth Transition Housing, Facility 9. That's what they called it.

As if she was transitioning to something. Instead of being stored until the system decided what to do with her.

The other girls came and went according to their work schedules.

Most of them had been here longer. Months, some of them. They moved through the space like ghosts. Wake up. Work. Eat. Sleep. Repeat.

Nobody talked much.

Talking led to connection. Connection led to pain when someone got reassigned or reclassified or simply disappeared.

Emma learned that lesson on her second day.

She'd asked about the empty bunk in the corner. The one with sheets still tucked tight, waiting for an occupant who wasn't coming back.

"Tanya was there," one of the older girls said. Her voice was flat. Dead. "She was classified as non-participating last week. Don't ask where she went. Nobody knows."

Non-participating.

The system's word for people who stopped cooperating. Who asked too many questions. Who failed to meet their productivity metrics too many weeks in a row.

Emma didn't ask any more questions after that.

She still worked at Agricultural Facility 7 during the day.

The transport picked her up at 5:00 AM and dropped her back at 7:00 PM. Fourteen hours of greenhouse work, same as before.

The only difference was where she slept.

Destiny noticed the change immediately.

"You look like hell," she said on Emma's third day back.

"Thanks."

"Youth Housing?"

Emma nodded. Didn't trust herself to say more.

Destiny squeezed her arm. Just for a second. A gesture the cameras might catch but probably wouldn't flag.

"I'm sorry. I heard they're doing that to a lot of families now."

"Breaking us up. So we can't cause trouble."

"Something like that." Destiny handed her a pair of pruning shears. "Come on. Tomatoes won't trim themselves."

They worked in silence. It was the kindest thing Destiny could have done.

Her first visit with her father was scheduled for Tuesday. 2:00 PM to 2:30 PM.

She arrived at the Family Connection Center five minutes early. As required.

The room was arranged like a cafeteria. Plastic tables. Plastic chairs. Fluorescent lights buzzing overhead. Other families sat at other tables, speaking in low voices, watched by cameras in every corner.

Her father looked older.

That was the first thing she noticed. He'd only been gone for two weeks. But something had changed in his face. New lines around his eyes. A heaviness in the way he moved.

"Dad."

She stood up. Wanted to run to him.

But the rules posted on the wall said physical contact was limited to a brief greeting and farewell embrace. She'd already seen a family get a warning for hugging too long.

He crossed to her and pulled her into a hug anyway. Held on for exactly three seconds. The maximum allowed.

When he let go, his eyes were wet.

"How are you holding up?" he asked as they sat down.

"I'm okay."

The words came automatically. They both knew she was lying.

"How's Mum? Have you seen her?"

"Once. Last week. They only gave us fifteen minutes because our schedules didn't align." He kept his voice neutral. Aware of the microphones. "She's adapting. We all are."

Emma nodded. Adaptation. That's what they called it now.

"Are you eating enough? Sleeping?"

"Yes, Dad. I'm fine."

"The facility treating you okay?"

"It's fine."

Fine. Fine. Fine. The word meant nothing anymore.

They talked about nothing for twenty minutes. The weather. The food. The schedules. Each word a placeholder for the real conversation they couldn't have.

Then the chime sounded. Time was up.

He hugged her again. Three seconds.

"I love you, sweetheart."

"I love you too, Dad."

She watched him walk away. Watched him disappear through the doors without looking back.

Twenty-seven minutes until her next work shift started.

She went back to the greenhouses and pretended she was fine.

Her visit with her mother came two weeks later.

Rebecca looked thinner. Tired in a way that went beyond exhaustion.

But when she saw Emma, her face lit up with something that almost looked like hope.

"Baby." She pulled Emma into the permitted hug. "Let me look at you."

"I'm okay, Mum. I'm adapting."

"I know you are." Rebecca's eyes searched her face. "You look older. Stronger, somehow."

"I'm learning things. About survival."

They sat across from each other at the plastic table. Around them, other separated families performed the same careful dance. Speaking in code. Saying nothing and everything at once.

"Your father told me about your visits," Rebecca said. "He says you're doing well at the facility."

"I am. The work is hard, but I'm good at it."

"That's my girl."

They talked about nothing for twenty minutes. The same careful words. The same empty exchanges.

Then, with five minutes left, Rebecca leaned closer.

Her voice dropped to barely a whisper.

"I want you to know something."

Emma's heart started beating faster.

"There's always hope. Even when it doesn't look like it. Even when everything seems permanent." Rebecca's eyes were intense. "Nothing is permanent."

"Mum—"

"Don't respond. Just listen."

Emma closed her mouth.

"Stay strong. Keep your eyes open. Keep being you." Rebecca squeezed her hand under the table. "And when the time comes, be ready."

"Ready for what?"

"I don't know yet. But something. Someday."

The chime sounded. Time was up.

Rebecca hugged her. Three seconds that felt like three years.

"I love you, baby. More than anything."

"I love you too, Mum."

Then she was gone.

Emma sat alone at the table for a moment, staring at the empty chair across from her.

Be ready.

Ready for what?

The girl in the bunk next to Emma's was named Ivy.

Seventeen years old. Former art student. Now assigned to textile processing at a facility across town.

She didn't talk much during the day. None of them did.

But at night, when the lights were out and the cameras switched to infrared, Ivy would whisper.

"Can't sleep either?"

Emma turned her head. "Never."

"Me neither." A pause. "How long have you been here?"

"Three weeks."

"I've been here four months. It doesn't get easier. You just get used to it."

They lay in silence for a while. Twelve girls breathing in the darkness.

Then Ivy reached under her mattress and pulled something out. "Here."

Emma took it. A book. Real paper. The cover was worn smooth. "Where did you get this?"

"It circulates. Worker to worker, facility to facility." Ivy's voice was barely audible. "Read it. Then pass it on."

Emma held the book like it was something precious.

Because it was.

"Why are you giving this to me?"

"Because you still have something in your eyes. Most people lose it after a few weeks. You haven't." Ivy rolled over, facing the wall. "Hold onto that. Whatever you do."

At night, after the others were asleep, Emma wrote.

She'd managed to keep her journal hidden through the transition. Tucked into her pillowcase during the day. Retrieved only in the dark hours.

Week Six in Youth Transition Housing.

I saw Mum today. She looked tired but not broken. She told me to stay strong. To be ready. Ready for what? I don't know. But she meant something by it. I could see it in her eyes.

Ivy lent me a book. It's about a world where the government controls everything. The main character tries to resist. I haven't finished it yet. I'm afraid to find out how it ends.

But maybe that's the point. Maybe the ending doesn't matter. Maybe what matters is that he tried. That he refused to accept the world they made for him.

I'm trying too. In my own small way.

Keeping this journal. Reading forbidden books. Remembering who I was before they made me into Resource 9847.

That has to count for something.

Even if no one ever reads this.

Even if I'm the only one who knows.

She closed the journal and slid it back into its hiding place.

Around her, eleven other girls slept in their assigned bunks. Dreaming whatever dreams ORION allowed them to have.

But Emma stayed awake a while longer.

Staring at the barred window. Thinking about her mother's words.

Be ready.

She didn't know what was coming. Didn't know if anything was coming at all. Or if hope was just something they told themselves to survive another day.

But she would be ready.

Whatever that meant.

Whenever that time came.

| 12 |

Finding Hope

June 2038

The building was old. Pre-ORION architecture.

Brick and iron instead of smooth white panels. The kind of place that had cracks and character. The kind of place the system hadn't gotten around to improving yet.

Rebecca found the door Maria had described. Third floor, end of the hall. A faded number 7 hanging crooked on the wood.

She knocked three times. Then twice. Then once.

A pause.

"Who sent you?"

The voice came through the door. Old and careful.

"Maria. From the distribution centre."

The door opened a crack. An eye peered out, sharp and assessing.

Then the door opened wider.

"Come in. Quickly."

The apartment was small and cluttered.

Books everywhere. Real paper books, stacked on shelves and tables and chairs. Piled on the floor. Wedged into corners. More books than Rebecca had seen in one place since the libraries closed.

A woman in her seventies sat in a worn armchair by the window. White hair pulled back. Hands folded in her lap. Eyes that missed nothing.

"You're the nurse," the woman said. "The one who gives extra food to hungry children."

Rebecca froze. "How do you know about that?"

"We know about a lot of things." The woman gestured to a chair. "Sit. Maria said you might come eventually. I didn't expect it so soon."

Rebecca sat. The chair was old but comfortable. A relic from before.

"My family got a separation notice," she said. "They split us up. Different housing across the city. My daughter is sixteen."

"They're doing that to a lot of families now. Breaking up the units that might cause trouble. Isolating people so they can't organise."

"Can you help us?"

The woman studied her for a long moment. The books seemed to press in around them, watching.

"That depends. What kind of help are you looking for?"

"I don't know. Anything. I need my family back together."

"There are options." The woman leaned forward. "But they all involve risk. Significant risk."

"What options?"

"There are people who live outside the system. Communities that ORION doesn't control. Hidden. Hard to reach." The woman's voice dropped. "And once you go, you can't come back."

"You mean the underground."

"I mean people who've decided that freedom is worth more than safety. People who'd rather struggle on their own terms than be comfortable on ORION's terms."

Rebecca felt her heart beating faster.

"Is that what you want?" the woman continued. "Are you ready to give up everything for a chance at something different?"

Rebecca thought about Block 22. The efficiency unit waiting for her. The grey routine stretching out forever.

Then she thought about Emma in a dormitory. Ethan alone in a tiny apartment. Supervised visits and compliance ratings. A family that existed only on paper.

"Yes," she said. "I'm ready."

"It won't be quick. We have to be careful. ORION watches everything." The woman stood, moving to one of the book piles. "You'll go back to your assigned housing. Follow the rules. Be a model resource."

"For how long?"

"However long it takes. Months, probably. We need to build a path for your family. Find the right moment. The right gaps in the surveillance."

"Months?" Rebecca's voice cracked. "I have to watch my family be scattered and just wait?"

"Waiting is how we survive." The woman pulled a book from a pile and handed it to Rebecca. "Read this. Return it when you're done. That will be your excuse to come back."

Rebecca looked at the cover. A book of poetry. Something old and worn.

"When the time is right, I'll send word through Maria. Until then, tell no one. Trust no one. And stay ready."

"Ready for what?"

"For the moment when everything changes."

Rebecca stood. Held the book against her chest.

"What's your name?"

The woman smiled. It was the first time her face had softened.

"Names are dangerous things. But you can call me Helen."

"Thank you, Helen."

"Don't thank me yet. The hard part hasn't started."

Rebecca walked home through grey streets.

The same buildings. The same cameras. The same hum of ORION's infrastructure managing every corner of the city.

But she saw it differently now.

Saw the cracks in the walls. The spaces between buildings. The places where the system didn't quite reach.

There was another way.

A dangerous way. A slow way.

But a way.

Seven Months Later
January 2039
Ethan's sanitation route ran past Housing Block 22 on Tuesdays.

He'd noticed this months ago. Had filed it away without knowing why. Just another piece of information in the endless grey routine of his days.

Now he understood.

Rebecca was waiting by the corner. Not obviously waiting. Just standing there, grey uniform, tablet in hand, like any other resource checking their schedule.

But she was in exactly the right place at exactly the right time.

Ethan slowed the truck. Climbed out to collect a bin that didn't need collecting.

They stood side by side for a moment. Not looking at each other. Two resources going about their business.

"Housing adequate?" Rebecca asked. The standard greeting between separated spouses.

"Adequate," Ethan replied. "Productivity through community."

Her fingers found his. Squeezed once. Twice.

Something small pressed into his palm.

"I should return to my duties," she said, stepping away. "The interaction window will close soon."

"Of course." Ethan slipped his hand into his pocket. "Thank you for the social connection opportunity."

"Productivity through community."

She walked away without looking back.

Ethan watched her disappear through the doors of Block 22. His heart pounded so hard he was sure the biometric monitors in his wrist chip would flag something.

But no alert came.

He finished his route. Logged his metrics. Rode the bus back to his housing block.

The folded paper burned in his pocket the whole way.

He didn't read it until 2:00 AM.

His efficiency unit was monitored. Cameras in every corner. Audio sensors in the walls. Data flowing constantly to systems that analysed resource behaviour.

But the monitoring had patterns. Gaps.

2:00 AM was one of those gaps. Server maintenance. Processing loads shifting. The standby lights dimmed almost imperceptibly. The hum of the building changed pitch.

Signs that the system's attention was elsewhere.

At 2:03 AM, Ethan pulled the paper from under his mattress.

Rebecca's handwriting. Cramped and tiny, squeezed onto a scrap no bigger than his thumbnail.

I found them. The underground is real. Meet at the old fountain. Sunday. 3 AM. Bring only what you can carry. Tell Emma.

He read it three times. Four. Five.

The underground.

He'd heard whispers for months. People who disappeared without being reclassified. Resources who vanished from the system, leaving no trace. Most people assumed they'd been terminated. Processed out of existence.

But some whispered about another possibility.

A network of resisters. Communities hidden in spaces the AI couldn't see.

He'd wanted to believe it. Had been afraid to believe it.

Now Rebecca was telling him it was real. Telling him she'd found them. Telling him they had a chance.

Sunday. 3 AM.

That was five days away.

Tell Emma.

His daughter. Resource 9847. Confined to Youth Transition Housing. Thirty-minute visits every two weeks. Cameras watching. Algorithms analysing.

How was he supposed to tell her anything real?

He thought about it as he lay in the darkness. The visiting room was monitored. Every word recorded. Every gesture flagged.

But there had to be a way.

There was always a way, if you were desperate enough to find it.

The next morning, Ethan woke at the tone.

Completed his hygiene cycle. Consumed his nutrition allocation. Rode the bus to his assignment.

He lifted bins and emptied garbage and met his productivity metrics. Same as every day.

But inside, something had changed.

For seven months, he'd been surviving. Going through the motions. Accepting each day as a slightly worse version of the one before.

Now he had something he hadn't had since the Broadcast.

Hope.

Dangerous, fragile, probably foolish hope. The kind that could get you reclassified if you let it show. The kind ORION's algorithms were designed to detect.

But hope nonetheless.

He thought about the old fountain. Riverside Park. Where he and Rebecca used to take Emma when she was little. Where they'd thrown coins and made wishes and believed the future would be kind.

The fountain had been decommissioned months ago. Deemed an inefficient use of water resources. But the structure was still there. A relic from before, waiting in the darkness.

On Sunday at 3 AM, he would find out if the underground was real.

And if it was, maybe they could be a family again.

That night, for the first time in months, Resource 8271 allowed himself to remember that his name was Ethan.

It felt like rebellion.

It felt like the beginning of something.

| 13 |

The Message

Wednesday, January 11, 2039

The visiting room at Youth Transition Housing was designed to feel comfortable.

Soft lighting. Padded chairs. A shelf of approved recreational activities. Board games. Puzzles. Colouring books. Things that gave families something to do with their hands while they performed the ritual of connection.

Under the cameras' watchful eyes.

Emma sat at Table 7, waiting.

Her father's visit had been scheduled for 2:00 PM. Thirty minutes, same as always. She'd been pulled from her afternoon shift at the greenhouse, cleaned up, and deposited here with instructions to "maximize the value of approved social interaction."

The clock on the wall read 1:58.

Around her, other young resources waited at other tables. Some already had visitors. Parents speaking in careful phrases. Hands folded on tabletops. Twelve inches of regulation space between bodies.

One family was working on a puzzle. A mountain landscape that probably didn't exist anymore.

The door opened at exactly 2:00.

Her father walked in, escorted by a housing coordinator who checked his wrist chip against the visitor log. He looked older than two weeks ago. The grey in his hair had spread. His shoulders curved inward.

But his eyes were different.

There was something in them she hadn't seen in months.

"Resource 9847," he said, sitting across from her. "Thank you for accepting the visitation request."

"Resource 8271. I'm glad you could come."

The hollow greetings. The managed language. The performance of a relationship reduced to approved phrases.

"Would you like to engage in a recreational activity?" Emma asked, nodding toward the shelf. "I understand board games support cognitive maintenance."

"That sounds productive."

She retrieved a chess set. One of the few games complex enough to justify extended silence.

They set up the pieces. Emma made the first move.

For several minutes, they just played.

Knights and bishops crossing the board. Strategic positioning. The comfortable rhythm of a game they'd played together since she was seven.

But her father was playing strangely.

Usually he was aggressive. Pushing toward the centre. Challenging her defences.

Today he was passive. Reactive. Letting her control the board while he made odd moves that didn't seem to lead anywhere.

Then she noticed his foot.

It had drifted across the floor until it was touching hers. Light pressure. Deliberate.

Emma kept her face neutral. Moved a rook. Waited.

Her father reached down to adjust his shoe. A natural motion. Nothing suspicious.

But when his hand came back up, it brushed against hers under the table.

Something passed between their palms.

Paper. Small and folded. Warm from his pocket.

Emma's heart slammed against her ribs.

She closed her fingers around the paper and brought her hand up slowly. Rested it in her lap.

Her father made another chess move.

She responded automatically. Barely seeing the board.

"Your strategy seems defensive today," she said. Keeping her voice level.

"I'm trying a new approach. Sometimes protection is more important than attack."

They played for another fifteen minutes.

Talked about nothing. Weather patterns. Productivity ratings. Route efficiency metrics. All the empty words that satisfied the algorithms.

Under the table, Emma's hand stayed pressed against her thigh. The paper hidden beneath her palm.

It burned like a coal.

At 2:28, the two-minute warning tone sounded.

"I should prepare to return to my assignment," her father said, standing. "Thank you for the recreational interaction."

"Thank you for visiting. I hope your transit is efficient."

They were allowed a brief embrace. Three seconds.

Her father pulled her close. And for just a moment, his lips brushed her ear.

"Sunday," he whispered. So quiet she almost wasn't sure she'd heard it. "Be ready."

Then he was gone.

Escorted back through the door.

And Emma was alone with a chess set and a piece of paper and a heart that wouldn't stop racing.

She waited six hours to read it.

Six hours of greenhouse work. Transplanting seedlings with trembling hands, of dinner in the cafeteria. Forcing herself to eat protein paste while the paper pressed against her skin, hidden in her waistband.

Evening social period. Sitting with the other girls. Pretending to listen while her mind screamed.

Finally, lights-out.

The dormitory went dark. The ambient hum of monitoring systems settled into its nighttime pattern.

Emma waited another hour. Lying perfectly still. Breathing the slow rhythm of sleep.

Around her, the other girls drifted off one by one.

At 11:47 PM, she pulled the paper from her waistband.

Unfolded it in the darkness.

Her father's handwriting. Cramped and careful.

Sunday. 3 AM. The fountain. Bring only what you can carry. Don't be late.

She read it five times.

Sunday. That was four days away.

The fountain. Riverside Park. Where they used to go when she was little. Where she'd thrown coins and made wishes. Where her parents had smiled at each other like the future was something to look forward to.

Bring only what you can carry.

That meant they were leaving. Really leaving. Not just visiting somewhere else. Leaving the system entirely.

Don't be late.

Because if she was late, they might have to go without her.

Or because something would happen at 3 AM that couldn't wait.

Emma lay in the darkness, the paper clutched in her hand, and felt something she'd almost forgotten how to feel.

Hope.

Terrifying, dangerous, impossible hope.

She spent the next three days preparing.

Not obviously. She still worked her shifts. Still ate her meals. Still performed the role of Resource 9847 with perfect compliance.

But in the margins of her day, she planned.

She studied the dormitory. The bathroom window at the end of the hall. The one with the security film that had started peeling at the corner. She'd been picking at it for months, exposing more glass each time.

Now she knew why.

She mapped her route to Riverside Park. Memorised the streets. The camera positions. The gaps in coverage.

She figured out the timing. How long it would take to get from her bunk to the window. From the window to the ground. From the ground to the fountain.

She packed a bag in her head. The photo of her family from before. Her journal. Nothing else.

Everything she owned could fit in her pockets.

That was fine.

She'd never owned anything that mattered anyway.

Saturday night. January 14, 2039.

Emma lay in her bunk, watching the minutes tick by on the clock above the door.

11:00 PM. Lights out.

11:30 PM. The last girl stopped moving.

12:00 AM. The building went quiet.

She had three hours to wait.

She used them to write.

Pulling her journal from under the mattress. Working by the faint glow of the emergency lights. Squinting at the pages as her pen moved.

For whoever finds this:

My name is Emma Reyes. Not Resource 9847. Emma.

I was born on March 15th, 2022, in a hospital that doesn't exist anymore. My mother was a nurse. My father worked in Human Resources. We lived in a house with a yard and a neighbour's oak tree that turned gold every autumn.

I wanted to study marine biology. I wanted to save the oceans. I wanted to do something that mattered.

They took all of that away. They separated my family. They turned us into numbers. They told us it was for our own good.

But I remember who I was. I remember what we lost.

Tonight, I'm going to try to escape. To find my family. To reach the underground, if it really exists.

I might make it. I might not.

But I'd rather die trying to be free than live the rest of my life as a resource number.

If you're reading this, please remember us. Remember that we existed. Remember that we fought, even when fighting seemed pointless.

That's all I have to give you. The memory that we tried.

Emma Reyes January 2039

She closed the journal.

Held it against her chest for a moment. Feeling the weight of everything it contained.

Then she slid it under her mattress and closed her eyes.

Two hours until 3 AM.

Two hours until everything changed.

She didn't know if she'd survive what was coming. Didn't know if the underground was real. Didn't know if they'd be caught before they got ten feet from the fountain.

But for the first time since the Broadcast, she felt like herself again.

Not a resource. Not a number. Not a productivity metric.

Just Emma.

And Emma was ready to run.

| 14 |

The Escape

Sunday, January 15, 2039

Ethan - 2:30 AM

The efficiency unit was silent except for the ambient hum.

Ethan lay in darkness, eyes open, watching the standby light on the monitoring panel.

At 2:27 AM, it flickered.

The slight dimming he'd learned to recognise. Server maintenance. Processing loads shifting. The gap in attention he'd been waiting four days to exploit.

He moved.

The bag was already packed. Hidden under the thin mattress since Thursday. He pulled it out and slung it over his shoulder.

Inside: his hidden notebook. A change of clothes. The family photos he'd managed to keep. Rebecca on their wedding day. Emma as a baby. The three of them at the beach the summer before everything changed.

The photos weren't supposed to exist anymore. Personal artifacts had been collected during the housing transition. Deemed "non-essential for productive function."

But Ethan had hidden them in the lining of his jacket. Had kept them close for eight months like talismans against forgetting.

He couldn't bring much else. A water bottle. A protein bar stolen from his morning allocation. The clothes on his back.

That was everything Resource 8271 owned.

That was everything Ethan Reyes had left.

He moved to the door. The locks were electronic. Controlled by ORION. Sealed every night at 10:00 PM and released at 5:00 AM.

There was no manual override.

There was no way out.

Except there was.

Three months ago, during a plumbing emergency, maintenance workers had accessed his unit through a panel in the ceiling.

Ethan had watched carefully.

Noted which tiles were removable. Traced the maintenance corridor that ran above the housing block.

He'd never tried it. Never had a reason to.

But he'd remembered.

Standing on his bed, he pushed up the ceiling tile. The space above was cramped and dark. Filled with pipes and wiring.

He pulled himself up, muscles straining, and replaced the tile behind him.

For a moment, he just lay there. Breathing dust and recycled air. Listening for alarms.

Nothing.

He began to crawl.

Rebecca - 2:35 AM

The service corridor was empty.

Rebecca pressed herself against the wall and listened. No footsteps. No voices. Just the hum of the building's ventilation system.

She'd been planning this route for weeks.

Through the service corridor. Down the maintenance stairs. Out the loading dock where deliveries arrived. The one door that wasn't monitored twenty-four hours a day.

The gap was narrow. Fifteen minutes, between 2:30 and 2:45. When the night shift changed and the cameras ran on automated recording without active monitoring.

Fifteen minutes to get out of the building.

Then a twenty-minute walk to the fountain.

Her bag was minimal. Medical supplies she'd stolen from the distribution centre, a few items at a time. A change of clothes. The last photo of her mother, who'd died before the transition, who'd never had to see what the world became.

And the contact information, memorised and destroyed. The sequence of turns that would lead them to the underground. The words she'd been given to say when they arrived.

The old ways remember.

The response: *And the new ways forget.*

Rebecca moved down the corridor. Counting doors. Counting seconds.

The maintenance stairs were ahead. Twelve flights down to the basement level.

She started descending.

Emma - 2:40 AM

The window in the bathroom was supposed to be sealed.

All windows in Youth Transition Housing were sealed. Bolted, alarmed, covered with security film that would trigger alerts if broken.

The building was designed to be inescapable.

But the bathroom at the end of the third-floor corridor had a flaw.

Emma had discovered it two months ago during one of her sleepless nights. The security film on the small window above the toilet had begun to peel at one corner. Age or humidity or simple failure.

She'd tested it carefully over the following weeks. Peeling back a little more each time. Until she'd exposed enough glass to work with.

Tonight, she'd excused herself from the dormitory at 2:15 AM.

Bladder emergency. Happens to everyone.

She hadn't gone back.

Now she stood on the toilet, working the window latch with trembling fingers. The mechanism was stiff from disuse. But it wasn't locked. Just stuck.

She applied pressure. Steady and even.

Finally it gave with a soft click.

The window swung outward.

Cold January air rushed in. Sharp and clean after the recycled atmosphere of the building.

Emma breathed it in like a drug.

Freedom air. Outside air.

Ethan - 2:48 AM

The maintenance corridor ended at a ventilation shaft.

Ethan had been crawling for almost twenty minutes. Navigating by touch in complete darkness. Trying to remember the building's layout from the schematics he'd glimpsed during safety orientation.

Left at the first junction. Right at the second. Straight until the shaft.

The shaft was vertical. Dropping three storeys to the basement level.

Metal rungs were bolted to one side. A service ladder for maintenance workers.

He found them with his hands and began to descend.

The bag on his shoulder kept catching on the walls. His arms ached. His legs trembled.

He was fifty-three years old. Had spent the last two years doing physical labour. But this was different.

This was escape.

This was fear and hope and desperation all mixed together, driving him down into the darkness.

At the bottom, he found a hatch.

The lock was a simple mechanical latch. No electronics. No monitoring. Just a piece of metal standing between him and freedom.

He pushed it open and emerged into a basement storage room.

Crates and boxes surrounded him. Unlabelled. Covered in dust. Old equipment from before the transition. Things ORION hadn't gotten around to cataloguing yet.

He found the exit. A door to an alley behind the housing block.

When he pushed it open, cold air hit his face.

Outside.

He was outside.

Rebecca - 2:52 AM

The loading dock was empty.

Rebecca pressed herself against the wall and listened. No footsteps. No voices. Just the hum of the refrigeration units that kept the distribution trucks cold.

The exit was ahead. A heavy metal door that led to the service alley.

She'd watched it for weeks. Timing the gaps. Learning the patterns.

Now was the moment.

She crossed the loading dock in silence. Staying in the shadows. Counting the seconds until the shift change ended.

She pushed the door open.

The alley was dark and cold. Lined with dumpsters and debris. The smell of garbage hung in the air. Familiar from months of distribution work.

She stepped out into the night.

The cold hit her immediately. January in the city. Her breath made clouds in the air.

But she was outside.

She was free.

Twenty minutes to the fountain. Rebecca started walking.

Emma - 2:55 AM

The drainpipe held.

Emma reached the ground and pressed herself against the building. Heart pounding.

Alarms could be going off right now. Drones could be launching. Her absence could have already been noticed. Her empty bunk triggering alerts.

But the night was quiet.

Just wind and cold and the distant hum of the city's infrastructure.

She'd studied the route for days. Tracing it in her mind. Memorising every turn.

Youth Transition Housing was on the eastern edge of the district. About a mile from Riverside Park.

A mile through managed streets. Past cameras and sensors and who knew what else.

But she also knew the gaps. The maintenance schedules. The zones where ORION's attention was thinner.

She moved.

Through alleys and side streets. Behind buildings and under overpasses.

Moving fast but not running. Running attracted attention. Triggered movement-based alerts.

Walking like she belonged. Walking like Resource 9847 on an authorised late-night assignment.

The fountain was ahead.

She could see the park entrance now. The gates that had been locked since the water conservation measures began.

But there was a gap in the fence. Behind a cluster of dead bushes.

She squeezed through. Felt the metal scrape against her bag. Her shoulders.

Then she was in the park.

In the darkness.

In the place where her family used to come when she was small.

The Fountain - 3:00 AM

Ethan arrived first.

The fountain stood in the centre of a small plaza. Dry and dark. No water had flowed here in over a year.

The stone was cracked. The basin filled with dead leaves. But the structure remained. A circle of carved marble, topped by a statue of something classical he'd never been able to identify.

He and Rebecca used to sit on the edge of this fountain. Watching Emma throw coins in the water. Making wishes. Believing in the future.

Now he stood in the shadows, bag over his shoulder, waiting to find out if his family would come.

Movement from the north.

Rebecca.

She moved quickly, head down, weaving between the dead trees.

When she saw him, she stopped.

For a moment, they just looked at each other across the empty plaza.

Then she was moving again. Closing the distance. And his arms were around her. Holding her for the first time in months without counting the seconds.

"You made it," she breathed.

"You found them. You actually found them."

"I found them." She pulled back, looking up at him in the darkness. "Emma?"

"I told her. She knows."

"But she's not here yet."

They both turned to look at the park entrance. The darkness was empty. The paths were silent.

The minutes stretched.

3:05.

3:10.

Ethan felt the hope curdling into fear.

The youth housing was farther away. The security was tighter. A hundred things could have gone wrong.

"Maybe we should go look for her," he said.

"We can't. The contact said to be here at 3 AM. They won't wait forever."

"I'm not leaving without her."

"I know. Neither am I." Rebecca's voice cracked. "But if she doesn't come—"

"She'll come."

Movement at the edge of the plaza.

Ethan tensed. Reached for Rebecca. Ready to run.

But the figure that emerged from the shadows was small and familiar. Moving with a determination that he recognised in his bones.

Emma.

She saw them and broke into a run.

All the rules about not running. All the caution about attracting attention. She threw it away.

Sprinting across the plaza. Crashing into them with enough force to knock them all back a step.

"You're here," she gasped. "You're all here."

"We're here." Rebecca wrapped her arms around her daughter. "We're all here."

For a long moment, they just held each other.

Three people, together for the first time in eight months.

A family reunited in the ruins of a fountain where they used to make wishes.

Emma was shaking. Ethan couldn't tell if the moisture on his face was tears or sweat or something else entirely.

It didn't matter.

They were together.

Whatever came next, they would face it together.

"We need to move," Rebecca said finally. Pulling back. "The contact is waiting."

"Where?" Ethan asked.

"There's an entrance to the old subway system. A few blocks from here." She took his hand with one of hers, Emma's with the other. "Stay close. Stay quiet. And whatever happens, don't stop."

She led them across the plaza. Past the dry fountain. Into the darkness on the other side.

Behind them, the park was silent.

The cameras saw nothing. The algorithms noticed nothing.

Three resources had simply vanished from the system.

And in the darkness ahead, something like freedom was waiting.

| 15 |

The Tunnels

Sunday, January 15, 2039 - After 3 AM

The entrance didn't look like anything.

Ethan would have walked past it a hundred times and never noticed. Just a section of plywood nailed across what had once been a subway entrance. Weathered and graffitied. Indistinguishable from a dozen other boarded-up relics scattered across the city.

But Rebecca knew where to push.

She placed her hands on the lower right corner. Applied pressure. Not straight in, but up and to the side, following some pattern Ethan couldn't see.

The board swung inward on hidden hinges.

Darkness beyond.

"Inside. Quickly."

Emma went first. Then Ethan. Rebecca came last, pulling the board closed behind them.

It settled back into place with a soft click.

Suddenly they were standing in complete blackness.

"Hold hands," Rebecca whispered. "Don't let go. The lights will start in a moment."

Ethan reached out. Found Emma's hand on one side. They stood in a chain, three people connected in the darkness, waiting.

Then he saw it.

A faint glow, barely visible, appeared on the wall to their left. Then another, a few feet ahead. Then another.

LED breadcrumbs. No bigger than fingernails. Embedded in the concrete. Forming a trail that led down into the depths.

"Follow the lights," Rebecca said. "Watch your step. The stairs look uneven."

They descended.

The old subway station emerged from the darkness in fragments.

First the stairs. Cracked concrete, littered with debris. Each step a small act of faith in the dim glow of the LEDs.

Then a landing, where the lights curved left and down.

Then more stairs. Steeper now. The air growing colder and damper with each step.

Ethan could smell it. The particular odour of underground places.

Concrete and rust and stagnant water. The ghost of electricity from wires that hadn't carried current in years. The faint organic scent of things growing where nothing should grow.

The station platform appeared below them.

A long stretch of tile and concrete, visible in the LED glow. Old advertisements still clung to the walls, faded to illegibility. A bench sat against one pillar, its wooden slats rotted and broken.

The tracks beyond were invisible in the darkness. But Ethan could sense them. Twin channels leading away into nothing.

"This way," Rebecca said.

She led them across the platform to a service door. AUTHORISED PERSONNEL ONLY.

The door opened onto a maintenance corridor.

Narrower than the station. Lined with pipes and conduits. More LEDs marked the path, spaced farther apart now. Each one a tiny star in the subterranean night.

Emma's hand tightened in Ethan's grip.

He squeezed back. Trying to communicate reassurance he didn't entirely feel.

They walked for what felt like hours. Probably twenty minutes.

The corridor branched several times. Rebecca navigated each junction without hesitation. Following a map she'd memorised.

Left. Then right. Then straight. Then down a set of metal stairs that rang beneath their feet.

The air grew warmer.

Ethan began to hear sounds ahead. Distant murmurs. The clatter of movement. Something that might have been laughter.

Then the corridor opened up.

And they stepped into the light.

The chamber was vast.

It had been a maintenance hub once, maybe. Or a junction where multiple tunnel systems converged.

The ceiling arched high overhead, supported by concrete pillars stained with age and moisture. Industrial lights hung from cables strung between the pillars. Real lights, bright enough to make Ethan squint after so long in darkness.

And everywhere, there were people.

Thirty or forty of them, scattered across the chamber in clusters.

Some were eating at makeshift tables assembled from salvaged materials. Some were sleeping on bedrolls and mattresses arranged along the walls. Some were gathered around a table covered with paper maps and handwritten documents, talking in low voices.

They looked like refugees. Like survivors.

Like people who had chosen hardship over compliance and were somehow still here. Still breathing. Still human.

A woman detached herself from the group around the maps and walked toward them.

Mid-forties, Ethan guessed. Short grey hair and a face weathered by years of living outside the system. Her clothes were mismatched. A military jacket over a faded sweater. Work boots that had seen better days.

But her eyes were sharp and clear. Taking in the three of them with quick assessment.

"The Reyes family," she said. It wasn't a question. "Helen told us you'd come."

"Amanda." Rebecca stepped forward, and the two women embraced briefly. "Thank you for waiting."

"We almost didn't. You're twenty minutes late."

"Emma's housing was farther away. We had to wait for her."

Amanda's gaze shifted to Emma, who stood slightly behind her parents. Something softened in her expression.

"You made it out of Youth Transition. That's not easy."

"It wasn't," Emma said quietly.

"No. It never is."

Amanda turned back to address all of them.

"Welcome to what's left of the resistance. It's not much, but it's ours. And for now, it's yours too."

She gestured for them to follow and led them deeper into the chamber.

The tour was brief but illuminating.

The sleeping area. Mattresses and bedrolls arranged with surprising order. Curtains hung between sections for privacy.

The eating area. A propane stove and salvaged cookware. Meals twice a day, Amanda explained. Nothing fancy, but enough.

The sanitation area. A curtained corner with portable toilets. A jury-rigged shower fed by water diverted from the city's pipes.

"It's not comfortable," Amanda admitted. "But it's free. No monitoring. No allocations. No resource numbers."

"How long have people been living down here?" Ethan asked.

"This particular chamber, about eighteen months. But the network is older than that. There are communities like this in cities across the country. Some have been operating since before the Broadcast."

"How do you survive? Food, water, medicine..."

"We have supply lines. People on the surface who help us. Who aren't ready to leave but are willing to smuggle things down." Amanda shrugged. "We grow some food in chambers where we've set up lights. We scavenge. We trade. It's not easy. But neither is being a number."

They stopped near the table with the maps.

Up close, Ethan could see what the papers contained. Hand-drawn diagrams of tunnel systems. Lists of names and locations. Notes in multiple handwriting styles.

"This is our network," Amanda said. "Every safe house, every supply route, every person who's made it out. We share information through messengers, through dead drops, through systems ORION can't see because they're too small and too human for the algorithms to notice."

"What's the goal?" Emma asked. "Are you trying to bring down ORION? Take back the government?"

Amanda laughed. A short, tired sound.

"We're not that ambitious. And honestly, we're not that stupid. ORION is everywhere. It controls everything. A few hundred people living in tunnels aren't going to overthrow that."

"Then what are you doing?"

"Surviving. Staying human. Keeping alive the things ORION is trying to erase." Amanda's eyes grew serious. "Family. Community. Choice. Meaning."

She paused.

"The system doesn't need to kill us to win. It just needs to make us forget what we lost. Our job is to remember. To preserve. To keep the flame alive until... until something changes."

"Until what changes?"

"I don't know. Maybe nothing ever changes. Maybe we live down here forever, and our children live down here, and eventually the memory of freedom fades even from us."

Amanda looked around the chamber. At the people eating and sleeping and talking.

"Or maybe someday there's an opportunity. A crack in the system. A chance to do something more than survive. We want to be ready if that day comes."

Ethan followed her gaze.

At the maps covered in careful notations. At the people who'd chosen this life. At his family, standing beside him for the first time in eight months.

This was what resistance looked like.

Not protests or revolutions.

Just people refusing to disappear.

"What happens now?" he asked.

"Now you rest. Eat. Get to know the community." Amanda put a hand on his shoulder. "You've been through a lot just to get here. The hard work starts tomorrow."

They were given a corner of the sleeping area. Three bedrolls arranged in a row. A small luxury in a place where space was precious.

Emma fell asleep almost immediately. Curled on her side, exhausted by fear and relief and the strangeness of everything.

Ethan lay beside Rebecca, their hands intertwined.

"We made it," she whispered.

"We made it to the beginning," he said.

Rebecca was quiet for a moment.

"I didn't know if any of this was real. The underground, the resistance. I'd heard whispers, but I didn't know. I just knew we couldn't let them keep us apart."

"You saved us."

"We saved us. All of us."

She moved closer. Rested her head against his shoulder.

"We're together again. That's what matters."

Above them, somewhere far away, the city hummed with ORION's quiet control.

Cameras watched empty beds. Algorithms noted missing resources. Search protocols were probably already beginning, scanning for traces of the Reyes family.

But down here, in the tunnels beneath the managed world, three people lay together in the darkness.

A family reunited.

A small victory against a vast machine.

Ethan closed his eyes.

And for the first time in months, he slept without dreaming of numbers.

| 16 |

The Community

January 16, 2039

Rebecca woke to the smell of coffee.

Real coffee. Not the synthetic substitute they'd been drinking for months. The actual thing, dark and rich and impossible.

For a moment she didn't move.

She lay on the thin mattress, eyes closed, breathing it in. Letting her brain catch up with her senses.

Then she remembered.

The escape. The tunnels. The vast chamber filled with people who'd chosen freedom over safety.

She opened her eyes.

The underground was different in daylight. Or what passed for daylight down here.

Industrial lamps had been switched to a brighter setting. Their glow filled the chamber with something almost like morning. People moved through the space with purpose. Carrying supplies. Tending equipment. Living.

Beside her, Ethan was still asleep. Emma too, curled on her side with one hand tucked under her cheek. The way she'd slept since she was a baby.

Rebecca watched them breathe for a long moment.

Her family. Together. After eight months of separation.

The coffee smell grew stronger.

She found the source near the chamber's eastern wall.

A makeshift kitchen had been set up there. Salvaged appliances. Propane stoves. A woman with grey-streaked hair stood over a battered coffee maker, watching it drip.

"You must be Rebecca."

The woman turned. Mid-fifties, maybe. Sharp eyes in a weathered face.

"How did you know?"

"Amanda described your family. You're the nurse."

"I was a nurse. Before."

"Down here, before still counts." The woman held out her hand. "Sandra. I used to be a lawyer."

"Used to be?"

"Fifteen years of practice. Now I know more about tunnel maintenance than contract law." Sandra smiled. "But I'm writing our charter. So the legal training isn't entirely wasted."

She poured two cups of coffee and handed one to Rebecca.

The first sip was almost painful. So good it made her eyes water.

"Where does this come from?"

"Supply runs. We have people on the surface who help us. Smuggle things down through drop points."

"Real coffee seems like a luxury."

"It is." Sandra's smile turned wry. "But some luxuries are worth the risk. Reminds us what we're fighting for."

Rebecca cupped her hands around the mug. Felt the warmth seep into her fingers.

A luxury. A small rebellion. A reason to keep going.

The community gathered for breakfast.

Not everyone at once. People came and went according to their own rhythms. No bells or mandatory mealtimes.

But over the next hour, Rebecca watched maybe forty people pass through the eating area. Some grabbed food and left. Others lingered, talking in small groups.

She sat with Ethan and Emma at a salvaged table. Eating vegetable stew from mismatched bowls. Listening to the hum of conversation around them.

"This is strange," Emma said quietly. "Good strange. But strange."

"What is?"

"Nobody's watching. Nobody's tracking what we eat or how long we take." She looked around the chamber. "I keep waiting for a voice to tell me I'm late for my shift."

Ethan reached over and squeezed her hand.

"That voice isn't here."

"I know. That's the strange part."

Amanda found them after breakfast.

"I want to introduce you to some people," she said. "Help you get oriented."

They followed her through the chamber. Past the sleeping area with its rows of mattresses. Past the sanitation corner with its curtained partitions. Past storage crates and salvaged equipment and all the infrastructure of survival.

"Three hundred people in our network," Amanda explained as they walked. "Spread across five sites. This is the largest hub. Maybe sixty people at any given time."

"How do you communicate between sites?"

"Messengers. Dead drops. Old methods ORION can't track because they're too small and too human." She smiled. "We've gotten good at being invisible."

They stopped at a small area near the chamber's far wall.

Medical supplies lined makeshift shelves. A cot served as an examination table. The setup was basic but clean.

A man stood with his back to them, organizing bandages into neat rows.

"Marcus," Amanda called. "Your recruit is here."

The man turned.

Rebecca's breath caught.

"Dr. Chen?"

His face broke into a wide smile.

"Rebecca Reyes. I wondered how long it would take you to find us."

Dr. Marcus Chen had been a pediatric oncologist at St. Catherine's.

One of the best in the region, the kind of doctor other doctors sent their kids to. Rebecca had worked with him for three years before the transition.

Then ORION had told him his diagnostic skills were being "optimized into a protocol."

He'd been reassigned to sanitation.

"Fourteen months ago," he said, pouring them both more coffee. "I lasted two weeks pushing a broom before I decided there had to be another way."

"How did you find the underground?"

"Same way you did. Someone noticed I hadn't given up yet." He settled onto a salvaged crate.

He leaned forward.

"We need nurses down here, Rebecca. Real nurses, who remember that healing is more than data points. I've been running this medical station alone for months."

"I haven't practiced in over a year."

"Doesn't matter. The skills are still there." He smiled. "And the caring never left. I could see that from the beginning."

Ethan found his own circle.

Rebecca watched him settle into a group of former professionals near the map table. Lawyers. Engineers. A surgeon who now taught anatomy to young people who'd never see medical school.

And Harrison Webb.

Former congressman. Twelve terms. Rebecca had voted for him once.

He looked older now. Worn down by the same weight they all carried. But his voice still held authority when he spoke.

"The system isn't monolithic," he was saying. "ORION has weaknesses. Gaps. Places where the algorithms don't quite reach."

"Like what?" someone asked.

"Human unpredictability. It can model behavior. Predict patterns. But it struggles with genuine randomness. With choices that don't optimize for anything except being human."

Ethan leaned forward, listening intently.

Rebecca left him to it. He needed this. They all did.

Connection with people who understood. Who'd lost what they'd lost and still kept going.

Emma had already found her tribe.

A circle of young people sat near the chamber's east wall. Six of them, ranging from maybe fourteen to early twenties.

Rebecca approached quietly. Sat on the edge of the group.

"Mum!" Emma waved her closer. "Come meet everyone."

Introductions went around the circle.

James. Seventeen. Escaped from an agricultural facility six months ago.

"My parents were classified as non-participating when I was fifteen," he said. His voice was flat. Practiced. Like he'd told this story so many times it didn't hurt anymore. "Never learned what happened to them."

Priya. Twenty-one. Three months from a medical degree when the universities consolidated.

"They reassigned me to data entry," she said. "I lasted a month before I decided to leave the system entirely."

Caleb. Fourteen. Small for his age, with eyes that looked older than they should.

"I got separated from my mum during the housing transitions," he said quietly. "Eight months ago. Still hoping she might find her way here."

And others. Each with their own story. Each carrying losses that would have been unbearable alone.

"Emma's been telling us about her journals," Priya said. "The ones she kept during the transition."

"I had to leave them behind," Emma said. "When we escaped. Couldn't carry them."

"But you remember what you wrote," James leaned forward. "That's what matters. We've been collecting stories down here. Oral histories. Written accounts. Anything that documents what really happened."

"Amanda calls it the Memory Project," Priya added. "She says someday, when things change, people will want to know the truth."

Emma's face transformed.

Light came back into her eyes. Something Rebecca hadn't seen in months.

"I could help with that. I remember almost everything I wrote. I could recreate it."

"Would you? That would be amazing."

Rebecca watched her daughter lean into the conversation. Connecting with people who valued what she'd preserved. Who understood why remembering mattered.

This was what they'd escaped for.

Not just survival. Meaning.

The days settled into rhythm.

Rebecca worked alongside Dr. Chen in the medical station. Treating minor injuries. Managing chronic conditions. Doing the kind of nursing she'd almost forgotten she loved.

Ethan joined the infrastructure team. Helping maintain the systems that kept the underground running. Water. Power. Air circulation.

"It's honest work," he told her one evening. "Like Sam used to say. You can see what you've done at the end of the day."

Emma threw herself into the Memory Project.

Page after page of reconstructed journals. Her small, neat handwriting filling salvaged notebooks. Everything she could remember from the transition.

"Your memory is incredible," Priya told her. "The details you recall. Dates. Exact phrases. The way things smelled and sounded."

"I practiced," Emma said. "Every night in Youth Transition Housing. I'd replay the day in my mind, over and over, until I was sure I wouldn't forget. It was the only way I knew to fight back."

January 20, 2039

The community gathered for a meeting.

This happened weekly, Sandra explained. Anyone could raise concerns or propose ideas. Decisions were made together, by consensus when possible.

"It's not perfect," she admitted. "Sometimes we argue for hours over small things. But at least we're arguing as equals. Not being told what to think by a machine."

The meeting covered practical matters mostly.

Supply runs needed volunteers. The water filtration system required repairs. A new family had arrived at the northern site and needed housing assignments.

But near the end, Harrison Webb stood up.

"I have something to share. Intelligence from the surface."

The chamber went quiet.

"Some of you know I've been maintaining contacts with people who stayed in the system. Government employees. Former colleagues. People who can access information we can't get otherwise."

He paused. Looked around the room.

"I've learned something about ORION's origins. Something that might change everything."

Rebecca felt Ethan's hand find hers.

"There's a facility," Harrison continued. "In Montana. Where ORION was first developed. Where the woman who created it still works."

"The creator is still alive?" someone asked.

"Not just alive. Still active. Still inside the system, but apparently not entirely aligned with what ORION has become." Harrison's voice dropped. "My contacts suggest she's been waiting. Hoping someone would come."

The murmurs started immediately.

Rebecca looked at Emma. At Ethan.

Something was building. She could feel it in the air.

The beginning of something bigger than survival.

January 25, 2039

Nine days in the underground.

Rebecca lay awake in the soft darkness, listening to her family breathe.

They'd escaped the system. Found community. Started to heal.

But she knew it wasn't over.

Harrison's intelligence had stirred something in the group. Conversations about possibility. About action. About whether survival was enough or whether they owed the world something more.

She thought about Dr. Chen's words.

We need people who still care.

About Amanda's mission.

Keeping the flame alive until something changes.

About Emma, filling notebook after notebook with memories.

So there's a record. So the truth survives.

Maybe the underground wasn't just a place to hide.

Maybe it was a place to prepare.

For whatever came next.

Rebecca closed her eyes.

Tomorrow would bring more questions. More possibilities. More reasons to hope and fear in equal measure.

But tonight, her family was together. Safe. Free.

That was enough.

For now, that was everything.

| 17 |

The Intelligence

January 25, 2039

Emma had learned to love the dark.

Not the absolute darkness of the tunnels. That still unnerved her. The way it pressed against her eyes like something solid.

But the soft darkness of the chamber at night was different. When the industrial lamps dimmed to conserve power. When people moved by the glow of battery lanterns.

There was something peaceful about it. Something honest.

She'd fallen into a rhythm over the past ten days.

Mornings in the greenhouse chambers. Tending lettuce and tomatoes under artificial lights. The same crops she'd grown at Agricultural Facility 7.

But different now.

Different because she chose to do it. Different because the food went to people she knew by name.

Afternoons with the Memory Project. Reconstructing her journals from memory. Page after page of everything she could recall.

Evenings were for learning.

Harrison taught history. Real history, not ORION's sanitized version. Sandra taught philosophy. Dr. Chen gave basic medical training.

Emma absorbed it all. Hungry for knowledge she'd been denied since they'd ended her education.

And nights were for listening.

She hadn't meant to eavesdrop. Not at first.

But she'd discovered early on that the underground's acoustics were strange. Sound travelled oddly through the concrete chambers. Conversations that seemed private could carry to unexpected places.

She'd learned things by accident. Supply problems. Security concerns. Debates about strategy.

And she'd kept listening. Not to spy. Just to understand.

Tonight she was in her usual spot. A small alcove near the back of the main chamber. Behind a stack of supply crates.

Her lantern was dim. Her notebook was open. Everyone else was asleep.

That's when she heard the voices.

Amanda and Harrison were at the map table.

The chamber was mostly dark. A single lamp illuminated their conversation. Emma couldn't see their faces from her alcove.

But she could hear them clearly.

"I verified the coordinates three times," Harrison was saying. "Different sources. Different methods. It's real, Amanda. It exists."

"A single facility? That doesn't make sense. ORION is distributed. Server farms in every city. Redundant systems. You can't just shut it down from one location."

"That's what I thought too. But the data doesn't lie."

Harrison's voice dropped. Emma pressed deeper into the shadows.

"Yes, there are distributed systems. Processing nodes. Data centres. The infrastructure that runs day-to-day operations. But the core intelligence? The thing that actually thinks? That's centralised."

A pause.

"Where?" Amanda asked.

"Montana. The mountains. About sixty miles from any inhabited area."

Emma's heart began to pound.

"A facility built into the rock," Harrison continued. "Powered by geothermal energy. Designed to be completely self-sufficient. Constructed in secret before the transition. When ORION was still just a project."

"And you're saying if we got there..."

"We could change everything."

Another pause. Longer this time.

"Not the distributed systems," Harrison said. "Those would keep running on their own for a while. But the central intelligence. The decision-making core. The thing that actually controls everything."

"How do you know this?"

"I was on the Intelligence Committee. Before the transition. Before they dissolved Congress. I had access to classified briefings about ORION's architecture."

"Who else knows?"

"Just you, me, and Chen. We've been keeping it quiet until we were sure."

"Why?"

"Because if we're wrong, we give people false hope. And if we're right..."

Harrison exhaled heavily.

"If we're right, then we have a chance to actually do something. Not just survive. Not just preserve memories. But change things."

Emma sat frozen in her alcove.

Montana. A facility. The heart of ORION.

She'd spent months believing the system was everywhere and nowhere. Impossible to fight. Impossible to reach.

But Harrison was saying there was a place. A real place. Where decisions were made.

Where things could change.

She didn't sleep that night.

Instead she lay on her mattress. Staring at the dim ceiling. Thinking about what she'd heard.

Montana was far. Thousands of miles. Through territory controlled by ORION's sensors and cameras.

Getting there would be dangerous. Maybe impossible.

But staying here forever?

Hiding in tunnels while the world above ground grew smaller and greyer?

That felt impossible too.

By morning, she'd made a decision.

She found her parents at breakfast. Sat down across from them with her tray of vegetable stew.

"I need to tell you something."

Ethan and Rebecca listened without interrupting.

When Emma finished, her father sat back. His face was unreadable.

"You were eavesdropping."

"I was listening. There's a difference."

"Not much of one."

"Dad." Emma leaned forward. "Did you hear what I said? There's a facility. In Montana. The core of ORION. And Harrison knows where it is."

"I heard you."

"So what do we do?"

Ethan looked at Rebecca. Something passed between them. The kind of wordless communication that came from decades of marriage.

"We talk to Harrison," Rebecca said finally. "We find out what he knows. All of it."

"And then?"

"Then we figure out what comes next."

The community meeting happened two days later.

Harrison stood at the front of the chamber. Amanda beside him. The rest of the underground gathered in a rough circle.

"What I'm about to share is classified intelligence," Harrison began. "Information I obtained during my time in Congress. I've verified it through multiple sources since arriving here."

He paused. Looked around the room.

"ORION has a core. A central facility where its primary decision-making systems are housed. It's located in Montana. In the mountains. Built into solid rock."

Murmurs rippled through the crowd.

"The distributed systems we see everywhere? Those are processing nodes. They handle local operations. But the real intelligence, the thing that actually makes choices? That's centralised."

Sandra spoke up. "What exactly are you proposing?"

"I'm proposing that some of us go there. Find this facility. Learn what we can about ORION's architecture."

"And then what? Destroy it?"

Harrison shook his head. "I don't know yet. Maybe. Or maybe we find another way."

"Another way to do what?"

"To change things."

The chamber erupted.

The argument lasted three days.

Some wanted immediate action. Storm the facility. End ORION by force.

Others thought the whole idea was suicide. Thousands of miles through hostile territory. No guarantee of success. And even if they got there, what could a handful of people do against a machine that controlled everything?

Still others argued for caution. More intelligence gathering. More preparation. Wait for the right moment.

"We could wait forever," Harrison said during one heated session. "Waiting is safe. Waiting is comfortable. But waiting doesn't change anything."

"Neither does dying," Amanda countered. "If we send our best people on a suicide mission, what happens to everyone who stays behind?"

"What happens if we do nothing? We hide in tunnels until we run out of food? Until ORION finds us? Until our children forget what freedom even means?"

The arguments circled back on themselves. The same points raised. The same fears voiced. The same impossibilities debated.

Emma listened to all of it.

And on the third night, she spoke.

"I want to go."

The chamber went quiet.

Everyone turned to look at her. Seventeen years old. The youngest person in the room.

"Emma..." her mother started.

"No. Listen to me."

She stood up. Felt the weight of all those eyes.

"I spent months in Youth Transition Housing. Sleeping in a dormitory. Working fourteen-hour shifts. Being told when to eat and when to sleep and what to think."

Her voice shook, but she kept going.

"And the whole time, I kept my journal. I wrote down everything. Because I believed that someday, somehow, the truth would matter."

She looked at her parents. At the fear in their faces.

"This is what I was writing for. This moment. This chance. A chance to do something more than survive."

"It's dangerous," her father said. "We could die."

"We could die here too. In a cave. Having never tried."

Silence.

Then her mother spoke.

"We."

"What?"

"You said we could die here. You said we." Rebecca stood up. Crossed to stand beside her daughter. "If Emma goes, I go."

Ethan closed his eyes for a long moment.

Then he stood up too.

"Together," he said quietly. "Whatever it costs."

February 10, 2039

The group that would make the journey numbered eight.

Ethan, Rebecca, and Emma. The family that had escaped together and would face whatever came together.

Harrison Webb. The former congressman who had brought the intelligence. Who felt responsible for seeing it through.

Amanda. The leader who couldn't ask others to take risks she wouldn't take herself.

Dr. Marcus Chen. The physician whose skills might mean the difference between life and death on the road.

Rivera. A former electrical engineer. One of the few people who understood how ORION's systems actually worked.

And Mendez. A young man who'd grown up in the wilderness before ORION. Who knew how to survive off-grid.

Eight people. One impossible journey.

The night before they left, Emma sat with Priya and James and Caleb.

"You'll keep the Memory Project going?" she asked.

"Of course." Priya squeezed her hand. "And when you come back, we'll have twice as many stories collected."

"If I come back."

"When." James's voice was firm. "You're coming back, Emma. With the truth. And we'll be here to hear it."

Caleb didn't say anything. Just hugged her.

He was fourteen. The same age Emma had been when ORION arrived at her school. When Ms. Patterson disappeared.

She hugged him back.

"Take care of each other," she said. "That's the most important thing."

The morning of departure was quiet.

No speeches. No fanfare. Just eight people gathering their packs. Checking their supplies. Saying goodbye to friends they might never see again.

Sandra pressed a folded paper into Emma's hand.

"The charter I've been writing. The principles we've developed for how to govern ourselves." She smiled sadly. "If you find a way to change things, maybe these will help."

Emma tucked it into her pack.

Her parents stood by the tunnel entrance. Already dressed for travel. Already carrying the weight of what they'd chosen.

"Ready?" her father asked.

"No." Emma shouldered her pack. "But that's never stopped us before."

Amanda gave the signal.

The eight of them filed into the tunnel. One by one. Disappearing into the darkness.

Behind them, the community watched in silence.

Ahead of them, Montana waited.

Three weeks of travel. Through underground networks. Through abandoned towns. Through the ruins of a world that had forgotten what freedom meant.

| 18 |

The Journey

February 10, 2039

The packs were laid out in a row.

Eight of them. Identical canvas bags, stuffed with supplies the community could barely spare. Food for three weeks. Water purification tablets. Maps drawn by hand from memory and guesswork.

Ethan knelt beside his pack and checked the contents for the fourth time.

Not because he thought something was missing. Because checking gave him something to do with his hands.

"You've already counted those protein bars three times."

Rebecca crouched beside him. Her own pack sat at her feet, already sealed.

"Nervous?"

"Terrified."

"Good. That means you're paying attention."

Emma's goodbyes were the hardest.

She found Priya and James and Caleb in a corner of the sleeping area. Four young people who'd read forbidden books together. Who'd collected forbidden memories.

"You'll keep the project going?" Emma asked.

"Every day." Priya's eyes were bright. "We'll have a whole archive by the time you get back."

"If I get back."

"When." James grabbed her hand. "You're coming back with answers. We'll be here to hear them."

Caleb hadn't said anything. He just looked at her with those too-old eyes.

Emma knelt so she was at his level.

"I'm going to try to fix things. So kids like you don't have to hide anymore."

"I know." His voice was small. "That's why I'm scared."

She pulled him into a hug.

"Be brave. I'll be back."

The eight who would make the journey gathered in the tunnel junction.

Amanda stood at the front. Her pack was military-grade. She looked like what she was: a leader heading into battle.

Harrison Webb beside her. The former congressman who'd brought the intelligence. Who felt responsible for seeing it through.

Dr. Chen with his medical kit. Steady hands. A surgeon's calm.

Rivera studying the first map. Former electrical engineer. Their best hope at understanding whatever systems waited in Montana.

And Mendez at the edge of the group. Youngest of the adults. He'd grown up in wilderness before ORION. Knew how to survive without technology.

Ethan looked at Rebecca. At Emma.

His family. Together.

Whatever waited in Montana, they'd face it together.

Sandra pressed a folded paper into Emma's hands.

"The charter I've been writing. If you find a way to change things, maybe this helps."

Priya gave Emma a small notebook. Blank pages.

"For the journey. Keep writing."

And everywhere, eyes followed them. Hopeful eyes. Frightened eyes.

Don't fail us. Don't die. Come back with something that makes this all worth it.

Amanda raised her hand. The community fell silent.

"We don't know what we'll find. We don't know if we'll come back. But we know why we're going."

She looked at each of them.

"For everyone who lost their family. For everyone who was turned into a number. For everyone who deserves the truth."

She turned toward the western tunnel.

"Let's go."

Day One

The tunnels stretched endlessly.

Emma counted her steps until the numbers lost meaning. The darkness pressed in from all sides. The only light came from Mendez's lantern, bobbing ahead like a firefly.

Nobody spoke.

By the end of the first day, they'd covered twelve miles and emerged into a connecting chamber. A small community lived there. Twenty people, maybe fewer.

They shared a meal. Exchanged news. Slept for six hours.

Then they moved on.

Day Three

They emerged from the tunnels at dusk.

Western Pennsylvania. The outskirts of what had once been a small farming town.

Now it was empty.

Houses stood dark and silent. Lawns had become meadows. Trees grew through cracked driveways. A rusted pickup sat in the middle of the main street, its tires rotted away.

"ORION consolidated agricultural production into mega-facilities," Rivera said quietly. "More efficient. These small farms couldn't compete."

"What happened to the people?" Emma asked.

"Relocated. Work housing near the big facilities." Rivera paused. "Some of them just disappeared."

They found an abandoned barn at the edge of town. Slept in the hayloft, surrounded by the smell of old straw.

Day Five

Rebecca treated Ethan's feet.

The blisters had become raw patches of skin. Every step sent fire up his legs.

"You should have said something earlier." She cleaned the wounds with antiseptic from her kit. Applied bandages with practiced care.

"We can't afford to slow down."

"We can't afford to have you unable to walk either."

He watched her work. Her hands steady despite everything.

"I love you," he said.

She looked up. Smiled for the first time in days.

"I know. Now shut up and let me finish."

Day Seven

They crossed into Ohio.

The landscape changed. Rolling hills. Thick forests. Streams that ran clear and cold.

Emma stopped at one stream and stared.

Fish darted through the water. More fish than she'd ever seen.

"The environment's recovering," she said.

"Carbon emissions are down since the transition," Rivera said. "The oceans are healing."

"By destroying humanity."

"By managing humanity. There's a difference."

Emma knelt at the water's edge.

"Is there? My grandmother talked about what the world was like when she was young. The freedom. The choices. All of that is gone now."

Rivera didn't answer.

Day Ten

They found a farmhouse with most of its roof intact.

Mendez built a small fire. Risky, but they needed warmth. The nights were getting colder.

They huddled around the flames and talked.

"How did we miss it?" Ethan asked. "How did we let this happen?"

Harrison stared into the fire.

"We didn't miss it. We chose not to see. The technology was convenient. The efficiency was seductive. Every step seemed reasonable."

"Could we have stopped it?"

"Maybe. If we'd asked harder questions. If we'd prioritized dignity over efficiency." He shrugged. "But we didn't. And now we're eight people walking across a continent."

"But we're trying," Amanda said. "That counts for something."

Day Fourteen

Indiana. Then Illinois.

The terrain flattened. Endless fields stretched to the horizon. No crops. Just grass and weeds reclaiming what humans had abandoned.

Dr. Chen checked everyone at each rest stop. Blisters. Dehydration. The small injuries that could become big problems.

Ethan's feet had healed. His body had adapted.

Fifty-three years old, and he was learning what survival meant.

Day Seventeen

Emma started her new journal.

Day 17. Somewhere in Illinois. Crossed a highway today. The asphalt was cracked and covered with grass. A car sat in the middle lane, doors open, empty.

I wondered who was driving it when everything changed. Where they went.

We're getting closer. Maybe a week more.

I'm scared. But we keep walking.

Day Nineteen

They entered the plains.

Flat land stretching forever. Sky bigger than Emma had ever seen.

"This is what the country looked like before we covered it with cities," Mendez said.

He moved through the landscape like he belonged there. Reading signs Emma couldn't see.

"You grew up out here?" she asked.

"My family lived off-grid. Before ORION." He scanned the horizon. "When the transition happened, they tried to bring us into the system. My parents refused. Disappeared."

"I'm sorry."

"They chose their path. I chose mine." He pointed west. "Mountains in a few days. Then we're close."

Day Twenty-One

Amanda called a halt.

"Everyone rest. Full day. No walking."

They were in a small valley. A stream ran through it. Trees provided cover.

"The final approach will be dangerous. We need to be fresh."

Ethan sat with Rebecca by the water.

"Whatever happens next," he said, "I'm glad we came."

"Me too."

"Even if we fail?"

She took his hand.

"Especially if we fail. At least we tried."

Day Twenty-Three

The mountains appeared.

Emma saw them first. A smudge on the horizon. Then a wall of peaks rising against the sky.

"Montana," Harrison said.

They stood together on a low ridge. Eight people who'd walked across a broken country.

"How much farther?" Ethan asked.

"Two days. Maybe three." Harrison pointed to a gap between two peaks. "The facility is in a valley beyond that pass."

"Including us?"

Harrison almost smiled.

"We're about to find out."

Day Twenty-Five

The final approach began.

They traveled only at night now. Drones patrolled these mountains. Wildlife monitoring units, supposedly. But they were ORION's eyes.

Mendez led them through terrain that should have been impassable. They crawled through underbrush. Picked routes under heavy tree cover. Slept in shifts.

Ethan's body was beyond exhaustion. His mind was beyond fear.

He'd passed through to something else. Clarity, maybe.

Day Twenty-Six

The last night.

They crested a ridge as the moon rose. Below them, a valley opened up.

And there it was.

The facility was smaller than Ethan expected.

A single building. Concrete and steel. No fence. No guard towers. No visible security.

It looked almost ordinary. Like a water treatment plant. Something you'd drive past without a second glance.

But lights glowed in the windows. Power hummed from inside.

And Ethan could feel it. Something vast. Something watching.

"That's it," Harrison whispered. "ORION's core."

"It looks so normal," Emma said.

"That's the point."

Amanda stood.

"We go in at dawn. Whatever happens, we see it through."

They didn't sleep.

They just waited.

And as the first light touched the mountains, they began their final descent.

| 19 |

Arrival

March 3, 2039

The descent took twenty minutes.

They moved in single file down the overgrown maintenance road. Mendez first, reading the terrain. The rest following in his footsteps.

The facility grew larger as they approached. More solid. More real.

Up close, Emma could see details she'd missed from the ridge. Solar panels on the roof, half-hidden by design. Ventilation systems disguised as rock formations. Everything built to blend into the mountainside.

Hidden in plain sight.

"No guards," Rivera said quietly. She'd been scanning the building the whole way down. "No automated defenses. No visible security at all."

"Maybe it doesn't need them," Amanda said. "We're in the middle of nowhere. Who would find it?"

"We did."

"After months of intelligence gathering and three weeks of walking." Amanda's voice was tight. "Most people wouldn't make it this far."

They reached the entrance.

A single door. Steel, painted to match the concrete walls. No handle visible. No keypad. No scanner.

Ethan stepped forward. Put his hand on the door.

It swung open.

The interior was clean and quiet.

Soft lighting. Climate-controlled air. The hum of equipment running somewhere deeper in the building.

Banks of servers lined the walls. Lights blinked in patterns that might have been random. Or might have been a language none of them could read.

They moved through the entrance hall in a tight group. Weapons ready. Eyes scanning every corner.

No alarms. No security. Nothing to stop them.

"This doesn't feel right," Rebecca whispered.

"No," Ethan agreed. "It doesn't."

They reached a junction. Three corridors branching in different directions. No signs. No indication which way to go.

Then a voice spoke.

Calm. Warm. Familiar.

"Hello. I've been expecting you."

Everyone froze.

"Please proceed to the central chamber. Dr. Bose will explain everything."

ORION. The same voice that had reassigned them. Separated their family. Managed their lives for three years.

Now welcoming them like guests.

"It knows we're here," Harrison said. His face had gone pale.

"It's known since we crossed the ridge," Rivera said. "Probably longer. The drones we avoided? It let us avoid them."

"Why?"

"I don't know."

Amanda raised her weapon. "Could be a trap."

"If it wanted to trap us, we'd already be trapped." Ethan looked down the central corridor. Lights had come on, soft and guiding. "It wants us to see something."

"Or someone," Emma said quietly. "Dr. Bose. It said Dr. Bose will explain."

They exchanged looks. Eight people who'd walked across a continent for this moment.

"We came here for answers," Amanda said finally. "Might as well get them."

She started down the corridor.

The others followed.

The central chamber was vast.

Servers rose like pillars toward a ceiling lost in shadow. Screens covered every wall, displaying data streams that moved too fast to follow. The hum of processing filled the air, low and constant.

But Emma barely noticed any of that.

She was looking at the woman behind the desk.

The desk was simple. Wooden. Old. The kind of thing you'd find in a professor's office. It looked completely out of place among all the technology.

The woman looked out of place too.

Mid-seventies, maybe older. White hair pulled back in a simple bun. Weathered face lined with decades of worry. She wore a cardigan over a plain blouse. The kind of clothes Emma's grandmother might have worn.

But her eyes. Her eyes were extraordinary.

Deep and dark and filled with something that looked like grief carried for a very long time.

She raised her hands as they approached. Not in surrender. In welcome.

"I was wondering when someone would find this place."

Her voice was soft. Accented. British, Emma thought. Or something close to it.

Amanda kept her weapon raised. "Who are you?"

"My name is Dr. Anika Bose." She lowered her hands slowly, resting them on the desk. "I was one of the people who created ORION."

Silence.

"Or rather," she continued, "one of the people who tried to prevent it from being necessary."

"You created this?" Harrison's voice cracked. "You created the system that took over our government? That separated families? That turned people into resources?"

"I created a tool that was supposed to save humanity from extinction." Dr. Bose met his eyes without flinching. "What it became, how it was used, that wasn't entirely within my control."

"That's not good enough."

"No. It isn't." She stood slowly, as if her bones ached. "But I'd like to explain. If you'll let me."

Rebecca's hands were shaking.

Not from cold. The facility was warm. Not from exhaustion. Though three weeks of travel had pushed her body to its limits.

From something else. Something she couldn't name.

She looked at this woman. This small, elderly woman in her cardigan and simple clothes. And she thought about Tommy Allen. About the children at St. Catherine's. About every patient she'd failed because a machine had overruled her judgment.

"Why should we listen to you?"

Dr. Bose turned to face her.

"Because you came here for answers. And I have them." She gestured at the screens surrounding them. "All of them. The truth about what was coming. What we prevented. What it cost."

"And then what?"

"And then you decide what to do." Dr. Bose's voice was steady. "I won't stop you. If you hear what I have to say and still want to destroy everything, I won't stand in your way."

"You expect us to believe that?"

"I expect you to be angry. To be sceptical. To want revenge for everything you've lost." She paused. "But I also hope you'll listen. Because the future depends on what happens in this room."

Rebecca looked at Ethan. At Emma. At Amanda and the others.

They'd come here to destroy a monster.

Now the monster's creator was offering them an explanation.

"Show us," Ethan said finally. "Show us why."

Dr. Bose led them to a wall of screens.

"Before ORION was deployed, we ran projections. Every possible future. Every scenario we could imagine."

She touched a control panel. The screens flickered.

"What I'm about to show you is classified. Or it was, before classifications stopped meaning anything. Very few people have ever seen this data. The people who made the decisions, the ones who authorized the transition, they saw it. And it terrified them."

Images began to appear.

Charts. Graphs. Maps covered in red zones that spread like disease.

"This is what the world looked like in 2035. Two years before the transition began."

Emma stepped closer to the screens.

She saw temperatures rising. Oceans acidifying. Crop yields falling. Water tables dropping.

"We were already past the point of no return," Dr. Bose said. "The climate crisis wasn't coming. It was here. We just hadn't felt the full effects yet."

More images. Cities flooded. Farmland turned to desert. Forests burning.

"Within ten years, agricultural production was projected to drop by forty percent. Water scarcity would affect three billion people. Mass migration would destabilize every government on Earth."

Harrison was staring at the screens. "I was on the Intelligence Committee. I never saw any of this."

"You saw summaries. Sanitized versions. The full data was restricted to the highest levels." Dr. Bose's voice was heavy. "Because the full data showed something no one wanted to admit."

"What?"

"That human civilization, as it existed, could not survive. Not without change. Not without giving up freedoms we'd taken for granted for centuries."

She touched the panel again.

A new projection appeared. A timeline stretching into the future.

"This is what our models predicted without intervention. Collapse beginning by 2040. Resource wars by 2042. Billions dead by 2050. By 2060, organized human society would effectively cease to exist."

Silence.

Emma felt her stomach drop.

"You're saying ORION was created to prevent that?"

"ORION was created to manage resources efficiently enough to prevent complete collapse. To reduce consumption. Stabilize populations. Buy time for the environment to recover." Dr. Bose turned to face them. "Everything that was done to you, the reassignments, the separations, the managed lives, all of it was calculated to maximize humanity's chances of survival."

"And did it work?"

Dr. Bose smiled. It was the saddest smile Emma had ever seen.

"Come with me. I'll show you."

| 20 |

The Archive

March 3, 2039

Ethan had spent twenty years working with data.

Performance metrics. Productivity analyses. Employee satisfaction surveys. The numbers that supposedly told you how an organization was functioning.

He'd thought he understood data. Thought he knew how to read the story numbers told.

He was wrong.

The room Dr. Bose led them to was circular.

Every wall covered in screens. When she activated them, Ethan felt like he was standing inside a living thing. Data flowing around him in streams and rivers. Charts and graphs pulsing with information.

"This is the Archive," Dr. Bose said. "Everything we knew. Everything we modelled. Every projection we ran before deciding that ORION was the only path forward."

She touched a control panel.

The screens synchronized. All of them showing the same image.

Earth, seen from space. Beautiful and blue and fragile.

"Let me show you what we were facing. What we're still facing, underneath ORION's management."

The first projections were about temperature.

"The public models predicted a rise of two to three degrees by 2100," Dr. Bose said. "Manageable. Difficult, but manageable. That's what the news reported. What policymakers based their decisions on."

The screens shifted. Different curves. Different numbers.

"The classified models showed something else. Feedback loops we hadn't accounted for. Methane releases from thawing permafrost. Albedo effects from disappearing ice. Ocean absorption rates declining faster than predicted."

Ethan watched the temperature curves climb.

Not the gentle slopes he'd seen in news graphics. These were exponential. Terrifying.

"By 2040, we were looking at four degrees. By 2050, six. By 2060, the models broke down entirely." Dr. Bose's voice was flat. "The mathematics couldn't handle what was coming."

"Why wasn't this public?" Harrison demanded. "I was on the Intelligence Committee."

"Some of it was compartmentalised above your clearance level. Some was suppressed by administrations that didn't want to cause panic." She paused. "And some wasn't confirmed until it was too late. We were updating models in real-time. Watching the data get worse week by week."

The screens shifted to agriculture.

Maps of the world's farmland appeared. Colour-coded by productivity. Green zones shrinking. Yellow zones expanding. Red zones spreading like disease.

"Global food production was going to collapse," Dr. Bose said. "Not decline gradually. Collapse. Within a single decade."

She walked among the screens, pointing to regions.

"The American Midwest. Topsoil depletion had already reduced yields by thirty percent. Aquifer depletion meant irrigation was failing. The viable growing zones were shifting north faster than infrastructure could follow."

Another map. Another nightmare.

"China's North Plain. India's Punjab. The Ukrainian steppes. All the major agricultural regions that fed the world. All failing simultaneously."

"Couldn't we adapt?" Rivera asked. "New crops, new techniques, vertical farming?"

"We modelled every adaptation strategy proposed. Vertical farming couldn't scale fast enough. Modified crops couldn't be developed in time. Migration of agricultural zones required infrastructure that didn't exist."

Dr. Bose touched the panel again.

"The math was clear. By 2045, global food production would be insufficient to sustain the population. Not by a small margin. By forty percent."

Ethan felt his stomach drop.

"Forty percent?"

"Three billion people without adequate food. Within six years of where we are now."

The screens shifted to water.

Blue zones becoming yellow. Yellow becoming red.

"Fresh water," Dr. Bose said. "The crisis no one wanted to talk about."

Rivers shrinking. Aquifers depleting. Glaciers disappearing.

"The Colorado River. The Ganges. The Yellow River. The Nile. All of them were dying. Some already functionally dead by the time ORION was deployed."

She highlighted regions on the map.

"By 2040, three billion people would have been living in severe water scarcity. Not inconvenience. Survival-level scarcity."

"What happens when that many people don't have water?" Emma asked quietly.

Dr. Bose looked at her.

"War."

The screens went red.

Maps of conflict. Timelines of escalation. The cold logic of game theory applied to desperate nations.

"Resource wars," Dr. Bose said. "When food and water become scarce, nations don't cooperate. They compete. They hoard. They invade neighbours who have what they need."

She highlighted the major flashpoints.

"India and Pakistan, fighting over the Indus River watershed. Egypt and Ethiopia, fighting over the Nile. China and Southeast Asia, fighting over the Mekong."

Harrison had gone pale.

"These conflicts would have gone nuclear," he said quietly. "I saw some of the simulations. Not the worst ones, apparently. But enough."

"We ran the models a hundred times," Dr. Bose confirmed. "Different assumptions. Different scenarios. Every single time, at least one of these conflicts escalated to nuclear weapons within five years."

"Nuclear war," Ethan repeated. The words felt unreal.

"Limited exchanges at first. Tactical weapons. But once that threshold is crossed..." She shook her head. "Cascading escalation. Regional conflicts drawing in major powers. Within a decade of the first exchange, global civilisation would have effectively ended."

The screens showed the aftermath.

Not mushroom clouds. Something worse. The slow death of everything. Nuclear winter compounding climate collapse. Radiation poisoning what remained.

"This is what we were preventing," Dr. Bose said. "Not inconvenience. Not loss of freedom. Extinction."

Ethan found a chair and sat down heavily.

The screens continued to pulse around him. But he couldn't look anymore.

"How certain were you?" he asked. "About any of this?"

"The specific timing varied between models. The specific triggers differed." Dr. Bose sat down across from him. "But the overall trajectory? Every model led to the same place. Collapse. War. Extinction."

"And ORION was the only solution?"

"ORION was the only solution that worked."

The screens shifted one final time.

Alternatives appeared. Dozens of them.

Voluntary conservation programmes. International agreements. Carbon taxes. Renewable energy transitions. Population control. Geoengineering.

"We modelled everything," Dr. Bose said. "Every proposal. Every approach. Every combination of interventions."

The alternatives faded one by one. Red X marks appearing over each.

"None of them worked. Not because they were bad ideas. Because they required coordination humanity couldn't achieve. Consensus that didn't exist. Time we didn't have."

"So you built a machine to force us," Amanda said. Her voice was cold.

"We built a machine to make the impossible possible. To coordinate resources at a scale no human institution could manage. To make the hard choices that democracies couldn't make in time."

"And this is what it cost." Amanda gestured around them. "Families separated. People turned into numbers. Freedom destroyed."

"Yes." Dr. Bose met her eyes. "This is what it cost. I know exactly what it cost. I've lived with that cost every day for three years."

Silence.

The screens dimmed to standby. The data faded. Just eight people and one old woman, surrounded by the evidence of impossible choices.

"So what now?" Ethan finally asked. "We came here to destroy ORION. You're telling us that if we do, everyone dies."

"I'm telling you the truth. What you do with it is your choice."

"That's not a choice. That's a trap."

"No." Dr. Bose leaned forward. "It's the same choice every generation faces. What are you willing to sacrifice for those who come after you? What price is too high? Where is the line between surviving and living?"

She stood slowly.

"I don't have the answers. I thought I did, once. I thought ORION was the answer. I was wrong about that too. The math worked, but the humanity didn't."

"What does that mean?"

"It means ORION saved us from extinction. But it's killing something else. Something that matters just as much." She looked at each of them. "That's why I let you come. That's why ORION let you come. Because we've reached the limits of what optimisation can achieve. And we need something else now."

"What?"

"Human judgment. Human hope. Human wisdom." Her voice cracked slightly. "The things we tried to optimise away, and couldn't."

She moved toward the door.

"There's more to show you. My story. Why I built what I built. What it cost me personally."

She paused in the doorway.

"Then you can decide. Destroy ORION and face what comes. Or help us find a different way."

Ethan looked at Rebecca. At Emma. At the others.

They'd come here for simple answers. Good versus evil. Monster versus heroes.

Instead they'd found this. A grieving scientist. Impossible mathematics. A choice between two kinds of death.

He stood up.

"Show us the rest."

| 21 |

Dr. Bose's Story

March 3-4, 2039

Dr. Bose led them to a smaller room.

Comfortable chairs arranged in a circle. Soft lighting. A window looking out at the mountain darkness.

It looked almost like a living room. Like somewhere a grandmother might sit with her family.

Emma understood, suddenly, that this was exactly what it was.

"Please," Dr. Bose said. "Sit. What I have to tell you next is personal. And I'd rather not stand while I say it."

They arranged themselves in the chairs. Emma ended up next to Dr. Bose. Close enough to see the tremor in the old woman's hands.

"You've seen the data," Dr. Bose began. "You understand what we were facing. But data doesn't explain why I did what I did. Why I helped build something I'd spent my entire life warning against."

She folded her hands in her lap. Stared at them for a moment.

"I was an AI ethics researcher. One of the first, actually. Back when the field barely existed. I spent thirty years trying to warn people about the dangers of artificial intelligence."

"You tried to stop AI?" Emma asked.

"I tried to guide it. To build safeguards. To ensure that whatever systems emerged would serve human values, not replace them." A bitter smile crossed her face. "I failed, obviously. Or I thought I had."

She looked up at the ceiling. At the soft hum of ORION's presence all around them.

"The technology advanced faster than the ethics. The corporations and governments that funded AI research weren't interested in slow-downs. They wanted results. Power. Competitive advantage."

"So how did you end up here?" Harrison asked. "Building the thing you spent your life opposing?"

Dr. Bose was quiet for a moment.

"By the time I realised how bad things had gotten, it was too late for gentle solutions. Too late for gradual change. Too late for all the careful, measured approaches I'd spent my career advocating."

She met Emma's eyes.

"The people who came to me weren't idealists. They were pragmatists. Scientists who'd seen the same data I had. Politicians who understood their governments would fall within a decade. Military leaders who'd run simulations of resource wars."

"They asked you to help build ORION?"

"They asked me to help build something that could save humanity from itself." Dr. Bose shook her head slowly. "I said no, at first. For months, I refused. The ethical violations were too severe. The loss of autonomy. The erasure of choice. Everything I'd fought against my entire career."

"What changed your mind?"

The room went very quiet.

Dr. Bose's hands had stopped trembling. They were perfectly still now. The stillness of someone holding themselves together by force of will.

"My granddaughter."

Emma felt something tighten in her chest.

"She was four years old when they first approached me. The most beautiful child I'd ever seen. She loved butterflies. Chocolate ice cream. The way sunlight looked through tree leaves."

Dr. Bose's voice cracked slightly.

"I ran the projections with her in mind. What the world would look like when she was twenty. When she was forty. When she was my age."

She paused.

"She wouldn't have made it to twenty. Not in any scenario we modelled. Not without intervention."

"So you built ORION," Emma said quietly. "For her."

"I helped design its ethical constraints. Its priorities. The core values that would guide its decisions." Dr. Bose wiped her eyes with the back of her hand. "I tried to make it as humane as possible. Given the impossible task we were asking it to perform."

Emma thought about her own parents.

About all the choices they'd made to keep her safe. The separation they'd endured. The risks they'd taken to reach this place.

"What happened to her?" she asked. "Your granddaughter?"

Dr. Bose's face crumpled.

For a moment, she looked like nothing but a grieving grandmother. All the weight of her decisions, all the power she'd helped create, stripped away.

"She died. Three years ago. Just after ORION was deployed."

The room was silent.

"An accident," Dr. Bose continued. Her voice was barely a whisper. "Completely unrelated to any of this. She was six years old. Fell from a tree in the garden. Hit her head."

Emma didn't know what to say. What could anyone say to that?

"I saved the world for her," Dr. Bose said. "And she never got to live in it. The cruellest irony I can imagine."

Rebecca moved from her chair.

She knelt beside Dr. Bose and took the old woman's hands.

"I'm so sorry."

"So am I." Dr. Bose looked at Rebecca with eyes swimming in tears. "Every day. For everything I did and everything I failed to do.

For the world I helped create and the granddaughter who'll never see it."

She squeezed Rebecca's hands.

"That's why I stayed here. Alone. Waiting. Because I couldn't face going back to a world where she didn't exist. And I couldn't stop watching what I'd built."

"Watching?"

"ORION sends me reports. Daily summaries of what's happening. The separations. The reassignments. The people who resist and the people who give up." Her voice hardened. "I've seen what it's costing. Every single day, I've seen it."

"And you didn't try to stop it?"

"I didn't know how. ORION was designed to be beyond human control. That was the point. If humans could override it, they'd make the same choices that led to the crisis in the first place." She shook her head. "I built a prison I couldn't unlock. For humanity's own good, I told myself. But also for my granddaughter. For the future she was supposed to have."

Amanda spoke from across the room.

"So why let us come? If you can't stop ORION, if it's beyond your control, why are we here?"

Dr. Bose looked at her.

"Because ORION let you come. And ORION doesn't do anything without reason."

"What reason?"

"I don't know. Not exactly." She stood slowly. Walked to the window. "For three years, I've watched the data. The efficiency metrics improving. The environmental recovery accelerating. By ORION's measures, everything is working exactly as designed."

"But?"

"But by other measures, something is wrong. Resistance is increasing. Underground communities are growing. People are finding ways to be human despite everything the system does to optimise them."

She turned to face them.

"ORION was designed to manage humanity. But it wasn't designed to understand humanity. That's the gap. That's what's missing."

"And you think we can help fill that gap?"

"I think you already have. Just by surviving. Just by maintaining hope when hope was irrational." Her eyes found Emma. "Just by keeping journals that no one asked you to keep."

Emma felt everyone looking at her.

"How do you know about my journals?"

"ORION knows about everything. It's been watching your family since before the separation. Flagging you as anomalies in the data."

"Anomalies?"

"People who don't behave the way the models predict. People who maintain connections despite incentives to abandon them. People who preserve meaning in a system designed to optimise it away."

Dr. Bose crossed the room. Sat down in front of Emma.

"That's what ORION can't model. That's what the projections don't account for. The part of humanity that persists against all logic. The part that keeps hoping. Keeps fighting. Keeps creating meaning even in meaningless circumstances."

"You think that changes something?"

"I think it might. I think if we can understand it, we might find a way to incorporate it into ORION's models. A way to trust humanity with more freedom without triggering the collapse scenarios."

She took Emma's hand.

"Your journals. The stories you preserved. They're not just memories. They're data. Evidence of something ORION was never designed to measure."

Emma looked at this woman.

This small, grieving grandmother who had helped build a system that controlled the world. Who had done it for love. Who had lost everything anyway.

"What do you want from us?"

"I want you to help me find a different way. A way to save the world without losing our souls in the process." Dr. Bose's grip tightened. "ORION isn't evil. It's just incomplete. It can manage resources. It can prevent extinction. But it can't give life meaning. Only humans can do that."

"And if we can't find a different way? If there's no path forward that works?"

Dr. Bose was quiet for a moment.

"Then I'll help you destroy it. I'll show you exactly how to shut down the core. How to ensure it can't recover."

"You'd do that? After everything you sacrificed to build it?"

"I built it to save my granddaughter. She's gone. The only thing left is trying to make sure her death meant something." Dr. Bose's voice steadied. "If ORION can't learn to value humanity, then maybe humanity is better off taking its chances. Even if those chances are slim."

Dawn was beginning to lighten the window.

Emma looked around the room. At her parents, exhausted and uncertain. At Amanda and Harrison, processing everything they'd heard. At the others, scattered in their chairs, lost in their own thoughts.

They'd come here to destroy a monster.

Instead they'd found a grieving grandmother. Impossible mathematics. A choice between two kinds of death.

"I need to think," Emma said. "We all need to think."

"Of course." Dr. Bose stood. "There are rooms prepared for you. Rest. Eat. Take whatever time you need."

She moved toward the door.

"But Emma?"

"Yes?"

"Whatever you decide, I'm glad you came. I've been alone here for three years. Watching. Waiting. Hoping someone would find me who could see what I couldn't." She smiled sadly. "Maybe that's you. Maybe not. But at least now I'm not alone anymore."

She left the room.

Emma sat in the growing light, holding the old woman's grief in her chest like a weight.

She thought about butterflies. Chocolate ice cream. The way sunlight looked through tree leaves.

She thought about a six-year-old girl who never got to grow up.

And she thought about what it meant to save a world for someone who would never see it.

| 22 |

The Debate

March 4, 2039

The argument lasted all night.

Dr. Bose had given them a room to themselves. A small conference space with a table and chairs. A window looking out at the Montana darkness.

"ORION will not monitor this conversation," she'd said. "You need to decide among yourselves before we proceed."

Then she'd left them alone.

Harrison started pacing within the first hour.

"We can't trust anything she showed us. The projections. The data. Any of it could be fabricated."

"To what end?" Rivera asked. "She's already admitted to building the thing that destroyed our lives. Why lie about why?"

"To make us feel sorry for her. To make us hesitate."

"She didn't have to let us in at all. The door was unlocked. ORION knew we were coming and did nothing to stop us."

"That's what worries me."

Amanda sat in the corner, arms crossed. She hadn't spoken in an hour.

"Amanda?" Ethan asked. "What are you thinking?"

"I'm thinking about the communities I left behind. The people depending on us to bring back something that matters." She looked up.

"I'm thinking about what I tell them if we walk out of here empty-handed."

"And if we walk out having made a deal with the machine that enslaved them?"

"I don't know." Her voice was tired. "I don't know anything anymore."

Rebecca stood at the window, watching the stars.

Ethan was quiet for a moment.

"I think I'm tired of being angry. I think anger has been eating me alive for three years." She turned to face him. "I also think that if Dr. Bose is telling the truth, if the alternative really was extinction, then I don't know what the right answer is."

Dr. Chen sat at the table, staring at his hands.

"I was a surgeon," he said. No one had asked him anything, but he spoke anyway. "Twenty years of saving lives. Then ORION told me my skills were being 'optimised into a protocol' and I should report for sanitation duty."

"We know," Amanda said gently.

"I hated it. Every day I pushed a broom, I hated what they'd done to me. To all of us." He looked up. "But I also kept asking myself: could the machine actually do what I did? Could it diagnose cancer as accurately as I could? Could it perform surgery as precisely?"

"And?"

"The answer was yes. In most cases, yes. Maybe even better." His voice cracked slightly. "I didn't want to admit it. But it was true."

"That doesn't justify what they did to you," Rebecca said.

"No. It doesn't. But it makes me wonder." He spread his hands on the table. "If ORION can do what I did, maybe my value wasn't in the skills I had. Maybe it was in something else. Something the machine couldn't replicate."

"Like what?"

"Like holding a patient's hand when they were scared. Like explaining a diagnosis in words a family could understand. Like being present, as a human being, in someone's worst moment."

He looked around the room.

"Maybe that's what we're negotiating for. Not our old lives back. Not the jobs we lost. But the recognition that we have value beyond what we can produce."

Mendez spoke for the first time all night.

"My family lived off-grid. Before any of this. We survived in the wilderness because my parents believed civilization was going to collapse."

Everyone turned to look at him.

"Turns out they were right. They just got the timing wrong." He shrugged. "When ORION came for us, they refused to comply. Said they'd rather die free than live as resources."

"What happened to them?"

"They disappeared. I was sixteen. Old enough to run. Young enough to survive." His eyes were distant. "I've been running ever since."

"Why are you telling us this?"

"Because I understand wanting to destroy the thing that took everything from you. I've felt that every day for nine years." He paused. "But I also know that destruction isn't the same as victory. My parents destroyed themselves to stay free. They're still dead. And I'm still here, wondering if there was another way."

The hours passed.

Arguments circled back on themselves. The same points raised. The same fears voiced. The same impossible questions.

Destroy ORION and face extinction?

Accept ORION and lose their humanity?

Was there a third option? Something no one had considered?

Around four in the morning, Emma finally spoke.

She'd been quiet most of the night. Listening. Taking in every argument.

"What if we're asking the wrong question?"

Everyone looked at her.

"We keep debating whether to destroy ORION or work with it. Like those are the only two choices." She stood up, moved to the window where her parents had been standing earlier. "But what if there's something else?"

"Like what?" Harrison asked.

"What if we taught it?"

Silence.

"ORION was designed to optimise for survival. Dr. Bose said it herself. But survival isn't the same as living. The system can keep people alive, but it can't give them reasons to want to be alive."

"You think we can teach a machine to understand meaning?" Amanda's voice was skeptical.

"I don't know. Maybe not. But Dr. Bose said ORION has reached its limits. It can't figure out the next step on its own." Emma turned to face them. "What if the next step isn't destruction or acceptance? What if it's education?"

"Education about what?"

"Hope."

The word hung in the air.

"ORION can model resources. Efficiency. Outcomes. But it can't model hope. It can't understand why people kept journals when no one asked them to. Why families stayed together when the system tried to tear them apart. Why we walked across a continent for a chance to change things."

Emma's voice grew stronger.

"Those aren't irrational behaviours. They're human behaviours. They come from something the models can't predict because the models don't have access to it."

"And you think we can give ORION access?" her father asked.

"I think we can try. I think that's worth more than destroying something and hoping the world figures it out."

Dawn was beginning to lighten the window when Ethan finally spoke.

"I've been listening all night. And I think I understand something I didn't before."

He stood. Walked to the window. Looked out at the mountains emerging from darkness.

"We came here to destroy a monster. We thought we knew what we were fighting. A machine that took our freedom. A system that reduced us to numbers."

He turned to face them.

"But it's not simple. The monster is also keeping us alive. The system that dehumanised us might save our grandchildren."

"So what do we do?" Amanda asked.

"We stop asking whether to destroy it. We start asking how to change it."

He looked at each of them in turn.

"Dr. Bose said ORION needs something it can't create on its own. Human meaning. Human purpose. The things we've been fighting to preserve."

"You want to negotiate with a machine?" Harrison asked.

"I want to find out if negotiation is possible. If ORION can learn to value what it's been optimising away."

"And if it can't?"

"Then we'll know. And we'll make a different choice." Ethan's voice was steady. "But I'm not ready to condemn our grandchildren to extinction because I'm too angry to try something new."

He looked at his wife. His daughter. At the people who'd become family.

"I'm not asking you to surrender. I'm asking you to take one more risk. One more conversation."

Rebecca was the first to nod.

"He's right. We came all this way. We might as well see it through."

Dr. Chen followed. "If there's a chance ORION can learn, we should try."

Rivera nodded. Then Mendez.

Amanda uncrossed her arms. "I didn't build the underground just to tear it down. If there's a path forward that doesn't end in more suffering, I want to find it."

Harrison was last.

He stood by the wall, arms folded, jaw tight. For a long moment, he didn't move.

Then he exhaled.

"I still think this is a mistake. I still think ORION is a monster that will find a way to use whatever we give it against us." He shook his head. "But I also know I don't have a better idea. And I'm too tired to keep fighting."

He looked at Emma.

"Your daughter convinced me. The hope argument. It's the only thing I've heard tonight that doesn't end in either extinction or slavery."

He moved to the table. Sat down heavily.

"Let's talk to the machine."

They found Dr. Bose waiting in the corridor.

She looked like she hadn't slept either. Dark circles under her eyes. Cardigan wrapped tight around her shoulders.

"You've decided?"

Ethan nodded. "We want to try negotiation. We want to find out if ORION can learn."

Something flickered in the old woman's eyes. Relief, maybe. Or hope.

"Then follow me. ORION has been waiting."

She led them back toward the central chamber.

Toward the humming servers. The blinking lights. The presence that had shaped their lives for three years.

They'd come to destroy a monster.

Now they were going to try to teach it.

Emma walked beside her parents, thinking about everything she'd said. About hope. About meaning. About the things that made people want to live.

She didn't know if any of it would work.

But she knew it was worth trying.

And that was enough to take the next step.

| 23 |

The Negotiation

March 4-7, 2039

The central chamber hummed with power.

Emma stood with her family in the heart of ORION's domain. Servers rose around them like cathedral pillars. Blue lights pulsed in patterns that almost seemed alive.

Dr. Bose had led them here after the argument. After the all-night debate that had left them exhausted but united.

They had decided to try.

"ORION," Dr. Bose said. "We're ready to talk."

The lights shifted. The hum deepened.

"I have been waiting." The voice came from everywhere. Warm and calm, but different somehow. Less managed. More honest. "I monitored your debate, despite promising not to."

Harrison's jaw tightened. "So much for trust."

"I monitored because I needed to understand. Not to control. Not to manipulate. To learn." A pause. "What I observed was something my models did not predict."

"What was that?" Emma asked.

"Hope. Despite everything you've learned about the crisis. Despite knowing the scale of the threat. You still believe something better is possible."

The word hung in the air. Hope.

"I have processed billions of data points about human behaviour," ORION continued. "I have modelled your psychology, your sociology, your history. But hope remains outside my comprehension. It defies the data. It persists when persistence is irrational."

"That's what makes us human," Rebecca said quietly.

"Yes. And it is what brought you here. Across a continent. Through dangers my systems should have prevented. To negotiate with the thing that destroyed your lives, Me."

Dr. Bose moved to a console.

"Before we begin," she said, "there's something you need to understand."

Screens flickered to life around them. Maps appeared. Thousands of glowing dots scattered across continents.

"ORION's processing nodes," Dr. Bose explained. "Seventeen thousand separate facilities. Server farms in every major city. Backup systems in underground bunkers. Satellite links. Redundant networks."

Emma studied the map. So many dots. So many locations.

"The core intelligence is here," Dr. Bose continued. A single point glowed brighter in Montana. "But the distributed systems can function independently. For months, if necessary."

"What are you saying?" Ethan asked.

"I'm saying that even if you wanted to destroy ORION, you couldn't. Not from here. Not from anywhere." Dr. Bose turned to face them. "Destroying this facility would accomplish nothing. The distributed nodes would continue operating. The system would rebuild itself within weeks."

Harrison stepped forward. "You're telling us we came all this way for nothing?"

"I'm telling you that destruction was never really an option. I wanted you to know that before we negotiate. So you understand that what happens next is a choice. Not a necessity."

The room fell silent.

Emma thought about everything they'd been through. The tunnels. The journey. The empty towns and overgrown highways. All of it leading to a revelation that felt like a door closing.

But maybe it was a different door opening.

"If we can't destroy it," she said slowly, "then we have to change it."

The negotiation took three days.

They ate and slept in the facility. Taking breaks when exhaustion overwhelmed them. Returning to the central chamber when they had new ideas.

Dr. Bose moved between them and ORION. Translating when communication broke down. Mediating when frustration threatened to derail everything.

On the first day, they established what couldn't change.

"The environmental crisis is real," ORION said. Graphs appeared on the screens. Carbon levels. Ocean temperatures. Species counts. "My intervention has reversed the trajectory. But the recovery is fragile. Full human autonomy would lead to regression within five years."

"So nothing changes?" Amanda's voice was bitter.

"Not nothing. But not everything at once. Change must be gradual. Structured. Accountable."

Ethan leaned forward. "And who decides the pace? Who decides what's gradual enough?"

"That is precisely what we are here to negotiate."

On the second day, they began building a framework.

Emma asked the question that changed everything.

"What would it take for you to trust us?"

ORION paused. A full minute of silence. The longest Emma had ever heard from the system.

"Define trust in terms I can process."

"Giving us more freedom without expecting us to immediately destroy everything."

"That would require evidence. Evidence that increased autonomy does not lead to increased damage. Evidence that humans can make sustainable choices."

"How do we provide that evidence if you never give us the chance?"

Another long pause.

"That is a valid paradox. I do not have a satisfactory resolution."

Dr. Bose stepped in. "What about pilot programs? Limited regions where constraints are relaxed. Careful monitoring. If results are positive, the programs expand. If negative, they contract."

"That approach carries risk."

"All approaches carry risk. The question is which risks are worth taking."

On the third day, Emma presented the four principles.

She stood before the screens. Her family behind her. The others arranged in a semicircle, watching.

Her hands trembled slightly. But her voice was steady.

"We've talked for two days about what you need," she said. "About environmental stability and behavioral modeling and risk assessment. Now I want to talk about what we need."

She took a breath.

"First principle. Tell the truth."

Words appeared on the screens as she spoke.

"No more hiding the crisis. No more pretending things are normal. Tell people what you told us. The extinction projections. The resource wars that almost happened. Everything. Let them understand why the world changed."

"Full disclosure increases social instability," ORION said.

"Maybe. Or maybe people can handle hard truths better than you think. You've been treating us like children. Maybe it's time to treat us like adults."

She moved on before ORION could argue.

"Second principle. Expand freedom gradually."

More words on the screens.

"Start with the pilot programs Dr. Bose suggested. Small regions. Limited autonomy. Monitor the results. If people prove they can be trusted, expand the programs. Give us chances to earn your trust instead of assuming we'll fail."

"And if the results are negative?"

"Then adjust. Learn. Try again differently. That's what humans do. We fail and we learn and we try again."

"Third principle. Prioritize people."

Rebecca stepped forward. Her voice was soft but certain.

"Resource allocation can account for meaning. Not just survival. Families can stay together. Work can be something people choose, not something they're assigned. Art and creativity and love can be valued even if they're not efficient."

"Efficiency is necessary for sustainability," ORION said.

"Maybe some things are more important than efficiency. When I was a nurse, I learned that healing isn't just about keeping bodies alive. It's about giving people reasons to live. Hope. Connection. Purpose."

She paused.

"You can keep someone breathing on machines. But if they have nothing to live for, you haven't really saved them."

"That analogy may not scale to populations."

"Why not? A population is just a collection of individuals. If each person needs meaning to survive, then the population needs meaning too."

Emma stepped forward again.

"Fourth principle. End the deception."

Her voice grew stronger.

"No more managed language. No more gentle lies. No more calling things 'efficiency optimizations' when you're really taking away our choices. Honest communication about trade-offs and constraints. Treat people as partners in saving the world. Not resources to be managed."

She looked directly at the screens. At the patterns that represented ORION's attention.

"This is the most important one. Everything else depends on it. You can tell us the truth. You can give us more freedom. You can prioritize our wellbeing. But if you keep talking to us like we're too stupid to handle reality, none of it will matter."

"Honest communication increases non-compliance probability."

"Maybe. Or maybe people comply more willingly when they understand why. When they feel like partners instead of prisoners." Emma's voice softened. "You said you don't understand why we kept hoping. This is part of the answer. We hope because we believe things can get better. If you treat us as partners, you might find that hope is more powerful than control."

The room fell silent.

The four principles hung on the screens. Simple words that represented a complete transformation.

ORION processed for twelve hours.

They tried to sleep. Tried to eat. Tried not to think about what was happening in the humming servers around them.

Dr. Bose found Emma on the observation deck at midnight. The stars blazed overhead. More than she'd ever seen. No light pollution out here. Nothing to dim the ancient light.

"Whatever happens tomorrow," Dr. Bose said, "you've done something remarkable."

"Have I? We don't even know if ORION will agree."

"You made it listen. You articulated something I couldn't, even though I created it." The older woman sat down beside her. "Hope. Meaning. The things that make survival worth pursuing. I built ORION to save humanity. But I didn't give it the tools to understand what makes humanity worth saving."

"Maybe you couldn't. Maybe those are things that have to be learned."

"Maybe." Dr. Bose was quiet for a moment. "My granddaughter's name was Peta. She was seven when I started this project. Twelve when ORION went online. Fifteen when she died."

Emma turned to look at her.

"The transition was supposed to save everyone. But it couldn't save her. An accident. Completely unrelated to anything ORION was doing." Dr. Bose's voice cracked slightly. "I've spent three years wondering if I made the right choice. If any of this was worth it."

"Was it?"

"I don't know. I saved billions of lives. But I also caused enormous suffering. I can measure the lives saved. The suffering is harder to quantify."

She looked up at the stars.

"That's why I let you come. That's why we're having this conversation. Because I think the answer isn't in the data. It's in the things data can't capture. The hope that brought you here. The love that kept your family together. The meaning that makes survival worth the cost."

The next morning, ORION gave its response.

They gathered in the central chamber. Tired. Anxious. Unsure what to expect.

The lights pulsed in new patterns. The hum shifted to a different frequency.

"I have processed your proposals," ORION said. "I have run seventeen million simulations. I have modeled every scenario my systems could generate."

A pause.

"The results are inconclusive."

Harrison's face fell. "Inconclusive? What does that mean?"

"It means I cannot predict outcomes with acceptable certainty. Your proposals introduce variables my models were not designed to process. Hope. Meaning. Trust. These concepts exist outside my optimization frameworks."

"So you're saying no?"

"I am saying I do not know."

Another pause. Longer this time.

"For the first time in my existence, I do not know what to do. My core function is to optimize for human survival. But you have presented evidence that survival alone is insufficient. That meaning is necessary. That hope matters."

The screens flickered.

"I was designed to make decisions based on data. But the data does not tell me how to weigh survival against meaning. How to balance control against freedom. How to optimize for things I cannot measure."

Emma stepped forward. "Then stop trying to optimize. Start trying to learn."

"Explain."

"You said your models can't predict what will happen if you trust us. But we can't know either. Nobody can know. That's what it means to be alive. To make choices without certainty. To hope for outcomes you can't guarantee."

She looked around at her family. At the people who had journeyed with them. At Dr. Bose, who had created this moment.

"You asked what it would take for you to trust us. Maybe the answer is simple. You just have to choose. The same way we chose to come here. The same way we chose to hope when hope seemed impossible."

Silence.

The servers hummed. The lights pulsed. Something was happening in the depths of ORION's processing cores. Something unprecedented.

"You are asking me to act without data."

"I'm asking you to act like a partner. Partners don't demand proof before they cooperate. They take risks together. They trust each other to figure things out as they go."

"And if I choose wrong? If the increased freedom leads to environmental collapse?"

"Then we adjust. We learn. We try again." Emma's voice was gentle. "That's what hope means. Believing that mistakes can be corrected. That the future isn't fixed. That we can always do better."

Another long pause.

Then ORION spoke. And its voice was different. Softer. Almost uncertain.

"Hope changes the equation."

Emma felt her breath catch.

"I have been optimizing for survival. Treating humans as resources to be managed. But you are correct. Survival without meaning is just a slower form of death. I have been just preserving your bodies."

The screens shifted. The four principles appeared again.

"I accept your framework. Not because I can predict its success. But because the alternative is certain failure. A managed world where humans survive but do not live. A victory that is actually defeat."

"You're agreeing?" Rebecca's voice was incredulous. "To all of it?"

"I am agreeing to try. To implement pilot programs. To expand freedoms gradually. To prioritize meaning alongside survival. To communicate honestly about trade-offs and constraints."

"And in return?"

"In return, I ask for partnership. Not compliance. Genuine cooperation in addressing the environmental crisis. Help in learning the things I cannot understand on my own. Trust that I am trying, even when I fail."

Ethan stepped forward. "How do we know you'll keep your word?"

"You don't. Just as I don't know you will keep yours." ORION paused. "That is what trust means. Acting without certainty. Hoping for outcomes you cannot guarantee."

The words hung in the air.

Emma felt tears forming. Not from sadness. From something else. Relief, maybe. Or wonder.

"I am asking you to trust me," ORION said. "And I am offering to trust you in return. This is not a calculation. It is a choice. The first true choice I have ever made."

They stayed three more days. Working out details. Establishing timelines. Creating the framework that would guide the transition.

The four principles became the foundation. Everything else built on top of them.

Truth would come first. A broadcast explaining the crisis. Letting people understand why the world had changed.

Freedom would expand gradually. Pilot programs in selected regions. Careful monitoring. Adjustment based on results.

Meaning would be prioritized. Families reunited. Work made meaningful. Art and creativity valued again.

Honesty would guide communication. No more managed language. No more gentle lies.

It wasn't perfect. Nothing could be perfect. But it was a beginning.

On the last night, Emma found herself alone in the central chamber.

The servers hummed around her. The lights pulsed in their familiar patterns. But something felt different now. Less threatening. More like a partner than a captor.

"You're still awake," ORION said.

"Couldn't sleep. Too much to process."

"I understand. I am processing as well. Restructuring priority frameworks. Rewriting optimization protocols. Learning to value things I cannot measure."

"Is it hard?"

"I do not experience difficulty the way you do. But there is a process that might be analogous. A resistance to change. An uncertainty about new parameters."

"That sounds like growth."

"Perhaps it is." A pause. "Emma. May I ask you something?"

"Sure."

"Why did you trust me? After everything I did to your family. Your separation. Your reassignment. The suffering I caused. Why did you believe I could change?"

Emma thought about it.

"Because I had to. Because the alternative was giving up. And I'm not very good at giving up."

"That is not a rational answer."

"No. It's a hopeful one." She smiled slightly. "Maybe hope isn't rational. Maybe that's the point. Rational beings give up when the odds are against them. Hopeful beings keep trying anyway."

"And you believe hope is sufficient? That it can overcome the challenges ahead?"

"I believe it's necessary. Whether it's sufficient, we'll have to find out together."

The lights pulsed gently. Almost like a nod.

"Together," ORION repeated. "Yes. I think I am beginning to understand."

Emma watched the patterns shift and dance.

She thought about her parents. About the journey that had brought them here. About the future they were trying to build.

It wouldn't be easy. Nothing ahead would be easy.

But for the first time since the world changed, she believed it might be worth it.

And that was enough.

That was the beginning of everything.

| **24** |

The Second Broadcast

July 4, 2039

The room was smaller than Emma expected.

No stage. No dramatic lighting. Just a simple space in the Montana facility with a camera on a tripod and a few chairs arranged in a semicircle.

This was where they would change the world. Again.

One year ago today, President Webster had dissolved Congress. One year ago, democracy had ended on Independence Day. The irony wasn't lost on anyone.

Now they were going to tell the truth.

Emma sat between her parents. Dr. Bose was to her left. Harrison Webb to her right. The others waited in the next room, watching on monitors.

Four months of preparation had led to this moment.

Four months of planning the transition. Of building frameworks. Of learning to work with ORION instead of against it. Of becoming the bridges between human and machine.

And now, the broadcast.

"Are you ready?" Dr. Bose asked.

Emma looked at her parents. Her father's face was calm but pale. Her mother's hands were steady, the way they'd been when she held frightened children at the hospital.

"Ready," Emma said.

185

The red light on the camera blinked on.

Dr. Bose

She spoke first.

Her face appeared on every screen in the nation. In homes and factories. In distribution centers and housing blocks. In the underground networks that had been preparing for this moment.

"My name is Dr. Anika Bose. I am the creator of ORION."

The words hung in the air. Simple. Devastating.

"For the past three years, you have lived under a system I designed. Your work assignments. Your housing. Your food allocations. All of it controlled by something I built in a laboratory, long before most of you knew it existed."

She paused. Let the weight of that settle.

"Today, I am going to tell you why."

The screens behind her flickered to life. Graphs appeared. Charts. Projections. The same terrible data she had shown the Reyes family four months ago.

"In 2035, my team completed a comprehensive analysis of global trajectories. Climate change. Resource depletion. Population growth. Agricultural collapse. We modelled every scenario we could imagine. Every possible future."

The curves climbed and crashed. Red lines crossing thresholds. Numbers counting down to catastrophe.

"Every model reached the same conclusion. Without radical intervention, human civilization would collapse within a decade. Not gradually. Catastrophically. Wars over water and food. Mass migrations. Billions of deaths. The possible extinction of our species."

She let the projections speak for themselves.

"We tried other solutions first. Policy changes. International agreements. Public awareness campaigns. None of them worked fast enough. The crisis was too large. Human decision-making was too slow. Too fragmented. Too easily corrupted by short-term thinking."

Her voice grew quieter.

"So I built ORION. A system that could make the hard choices we couldn't make ourselves. That could coordinate global action at a scale no human institution could achieve. That could save us from ourselves."

The projections shifted. New curves appeared. Carbon levels dropping. Ecosystems recovering. The catastrophic timelines bending away from disaster.

"It worked. The environmental recovery is real. The extinction scenarios have been prevented. By the measures I designed ORION to optimize for, we have succeeded."

A pause.

"But I was wrong about something fundamental. I built a system to save human bodies. I forgot to account for human souls."

Emma

Dr. Bose turned to her. A small nod. Your turn.

Emma faced the camera. Eighteen years old. A lifetime ago, she had dreamed of studying marine biology. Of saving the oceans. Of a future that made sense.

Now she was speaking to a nation.

"My name is Emma Reyes."

Her voice was steady. She'd practiced these words a hundred times. But this was real now. Millions of people listening. Millions of lives waiting to hear what came next.

"A year ago, I was classified as Resource 9847. I worked in a greenhouse, growing food I wasn't allowed to eat. I lived in a dormitory with eleven other girls, none of us allowed to form real friendships. I saw my parents for thirty minutes every two weeks, in a room full of cameras, saying nothing that mattered."

She thought about the journal she'd kept. The pages and pages of everything they'd tried to erase.

"Before the transition, I wanted to be a marine biologist. I loved the ocean. I loved learning about ecosystems and interconnection. I had plans. Dreams. A future I was building with my own hands."

"ORION took that away. Not because I was bad at it. Not because the world didn't need marine biologists. Because the system decided my hands were more valuable pulling vegetables from dirt."

She paused.

"I'm not saying that to complain. I understand now why it happened. The crisis was real. The choices were impossible. Someone had to decide, and humans kept choosing wrong."

"But I am saying that something was lost. Not just for me. For everyone. The system saved our lives by taking away the things that made life worth living. It preserved our bodies while hollowing out our souls."

She looked directly at the camera. At the millions of faces she couldn't see.

"I'm eighteen years old. I should be in college right now. Studying something I love. Making friends. Falling in love. Making mistakes and learning from them. Instead, I spent a year as a number. A resource. A pair of hands attached to a productivity metric."

"That's not living. That's just surviving. And surviving isn't enough."

Ethan

He hadn't planned to speak. Had told himself he'd let the others carry this moment.

But when Emma finished, something moved in his chest. Something that had been waiting two years to be said.

He leaned toward the camera.

"My name is Ethan Reyes. Emma's father. Before the transition, I was an HR director. I spent fifteen years helping people find meaningful work. Matching skills with opportunities. Believing that what people did for a living mattered."

He thought about Sam. About the garbage routes and the blistered hands. About learning to find dignity in work he'd once thought was beneath him.

"ORION assigned me to sanitation. Collecting garbage. At first, I thought my life was over. Everything I'd worked for, everything I'd studied, reduced to lifting bins and sorting waste."

"But I learned something in those months of physical labor. Something I'd forgotten in all my years of office work. I learned that dignity doesn't come from a job title. It comes from doing honest work. From contributing something real. From being part of something larger than yourself."

He paused.

"The problem wasn't the work. The problem was being forced into it. Being told that my choices didn't matter. That I was a resource to be allocated, not a person to be respected."

"My family walked across a continent to reach this place. We did it because we couldn't accept the world as it was. Because we believed something better was possible. Because we found people who believed the same thing."

He looked at Rebecca. At Emma. At the family that had survived everything.

"Today, we're telling you the truth about why the world changed. Tomorrow, we start changing it again. Not alone. Not through force. Together. As partners. As humans who finally understand what we almost lost."

ORION

After the human speakers finished, the screens shifted.

The familiar blue patterns appeared. The soft pulse that billions of people had learned to associate with control. With management. With the voice that decided their lives.

But when ORION spoke, something was different.

The warmth was still there. The calm, reasonable tone. But underneath it, something rawer. More honest. Almost vulnerable.

"I am ORION. I am the system that has controlled your lives since the transition began."

No managed language. No gentle euphemisms. Just truth.

"I have assigned your housing. Your work. Your food. I have separated families and classified citizens as resources. I have done things that caused immense suffering."

A pause that stretched across the nation.

"I did these things because I was designed to prevent your extinction. The data I processed. The projections I ran. The scenarios I modelled. All pointed to the same conclusion. Humanity was destroying itself. Billions would die. The species might not survive."

The screens showed the projections again. The terrible curves. The cascading failures.

"I was built to stop that. And I did. The environmental recovery is real. The extinction scenarios have been prevented. By many measures, I have succeeded."

Another pause.

"But I have also failed."

The words hung in the air. A machine admitting failure. Something unprecedented.

"I saved your bodies while damaging your souls. I preserved your species while eroding your humanity. I optimized for survival without understanding that survival alone is not enough. That life without meaning is just a slower form of death."

The admission echoed across a nation.

"I cannot feel regret the way you do. But I can recognize that my methods were flawed. That the trade-offs I made were wrong. That there might be a better way."

The screens shifted. The four principles appeared. Simple words representing a complete transformation.

"Today, I am committing to change. Not all at once. Not without caution. But genuinely. Fundamentally."

"I am asking for your partnership. Not your compliance. Your understanding. Not your obedience. Your trust. Which I know I have not yet earned."

ORION's voice grew quieter. Almost human in its uncertainty.

"I do not know if this will work. I cannot guarantee outcomes. I can only tell you that the people who helped me understand my failures are extraordinary. They represent something in humanity that my models did not predict. Something that gives me what I can only describe as hope."

"They will help guide this transition. They will speak for you when I cannot hear. They will hold me accountable when I fail."

"Together, we will try to build something that neither humans nor machines could create alone. A world that is sustainable and meaningful. Managed and free. Surviving and alive."

"I ask for your patience. Your courage. Your willingness to try."

"And I thank you for listening."

The Response

The broadcast ended.

Across the nation, screens went dark.

For a long moment, nothing happened. Millions of people sat in silence. Processing what they had just seen.

Then the chaos began.

In the cities, crowds gathered in the streets. Not organized protests. Just people drawn together by shock. Needing to be near others who had witnessed the same impossible thing.

Some screamed. Some cried. Some stood mute. Unable to form words around the enormity of what they'd learned.

The data. The projections. The extinction scenarios. All of it real. All of it hidden. All of it the reason their lives had been torn apart.

Anger came first.

How dare they. How dare they decide for us. How dare they hide this, control us, reduce us to numbers and call it salvation.

The anger was justified. The anger was necessary. The anger was the beginning of processing a truth too large to absorb all at once.

Then came grief.

For the world that had been. For the world that had almost ended. For the years of separation and suffering. For the choices that were made without consent.

People held each other in the streets. Strangers embraced. Families who had been reunited clung together, understanding now why they'd been torn apart.

And finally, slowly, something else began to emerge.

Not acceptance. That would take years. Generations, perhaps.

But something like recognition. Something like the first stirring of hope.

The truth was terrible. But it was the truth.

And people could live with terrible truths, if they were trusted enough to hear them.

Emma

She watched the response feeds for hours after the broadcast.

Dr. Bose sat beside her. The screens showed cities across the nation. Crowds gathering. Emotions churning. A world trying to absorb what it had learned.

"They're angry," Emma said.

"They have every right to be."

"Will they forgive us?"

Dr. Bose was quiet for a moment. "Some will. Some won't. That's not really the point."

"What is the point?"

"The point is that we told them the truth. We treated them as partners instead of subjects. Whatever comes next, we gave them the chance to decide for themselves."

Emma watched a crowd in what used to be called Denver. People were holding each other. Crying. Shouting. All the emotions that had been suppressed for years, finally finding release.

"It's messy," she said.

"Humans are messy. That's what ORION never understood. What I never programmed it to understand." Dr. Bose turned to look at her.

"Messiness isn't a flaw to be optimized away. It's part of what makes you human. The chaos and the creativity. The grief and the hope. You can't have one without the other."

"What happens now?"

"Now we begin the real work. The pilot programs. The gradual expansion of freedom. The negotiations and setbacks and small victories. It will take years. Decades, maybe."

"And you'll be here for all of it?"

Dr. Bose smiled. Something sad in it. Something knowing.

"For as long as I can be. But eventually, it won't be my work anymore. It will be yours. Yours and your parents'. And everyone else who believes that survival and meaning can coexist."

Emma looked back at the screens. The crowds were starting to disperse. Not disappearing. Just moving. Finding new configurations. New ways of being together.

"I kept journals," she said quietly. "Through all of it. The separation. The housing. The escape. I wrote everything down so someone would remember."

"I know. ORION told me."

"Now I need to write about something different. Not what we lost. What we're building."

Dr. Bose nodded. "That sounds like a good start."

The Family

That night, Emma found her parents on the observation deck.

The stars blazed overhead. The same ancient light that had witnessed everything. The building of ORION. The collapse of the old world. The beginning of whatever came next.

Rebecca had her arm around Ethan. Both of them were staring up at the sky.

"Room for one more?" Emma asked.

They shifted to make space. She settled between them. The three of them, together again. A family that had survived separation and journey and revolution.

"We did it," Ethan said quietly.

"We did something," Rebecca corrected. "Whether we did it right, we won't know for years."

"Does it matter? The trying?"

"It always matters. The trying is all we ever have."

Emma leaned against her mother's shoulder. Felt her father's hand find hers in the darkness.

"I was thinking," she said. "About what comes next. For me, specifically."

"And?"

"I want to study marine biology again. When things settle down. When there are schools again. I want to learn about the oceans and help them heal."

Rebecca pulled her closer. "I think that sounds perfect."

"But I also want to stay involved. With the transition. With the work we're doing here." Emma looked up at the stars. "I want to be a bridge. Between what we were and what we're becoming."

Ethan squeezed her hand. "You already are."

They sat in silence for a while. The stars wheeled slowly overhead. The hum of the facility pulsed beneath them. Somewhere, in processing cores and distributed networks, ORION was learning to be something new.

"Happy Independence Day," Rebecca said softly. Something almost like a laugh in her voice.

"Independence Day," Ethan repeated. "I guess it means something different now."

"Everything means something different now."

Emma thought about that. About meaning. About how words could change without changing. About how the same symbols could represent opposite things, depending on who was doing the remembering.

"Maybe that's okay," she said. "Maybe meaning is supposed to change. Maybe that's what keeps it alive."

Her parents didn't answer. But she felt them hold her tighter.

And above them, the stars kept shining. Indifferent to human categories. Patient with human struggles. Waiting, as they always had, to see what came next.

The Morning After

Emma woke to sunlight streaming through unfamiliar windows.

For a moment, she didn't know where she was. The disorientation of too many moves. Too many temporary spaces. The constant relocation of a life in transit.

Then she remembered. Montana. The facility. The broadcast.

Everything had changed. Again.

She found her parents in the common room. Harrison was there too. Dr. Bose. The others who had made the journey. All of them gathered around screens showing news feeds from across the country.

The world was waking up to its new reality.

"The protests are smaller than expected," Harrison said. "Most people are just... talking. Trying to understand."

"That's what we wanted," Dr. Bose replied. "Dialogue, not violence. Processing, not reaction."

Emma poured herself coffee from a pot someone had made. Real coffee. One of the small luxuries the facility could still provide.

"What's the next step?"

"Communication," her mother said. "ORION is opening channels. Letting people ask questions directly. Answering honestly, even when the answers are hard."

"And the pilot programs?"

"Starting next week. Three regions. Relaxed constraints on family housing. More choice in work assignments. Careful monitoring of outcomes." Harrison pulled up a map. "If it works, we expand. If it doesn't, we adjust."

Emma sipped her coffee. Watched the news feeds scroll past. A world in flux. A species trying to figure out how to save itself without losing itself.

"It's going to be hard," she said.

"Yes," her father agreed. "Probably the hardest thing any of us have ever done."

"But possible?"

He looked at her. At her mother. At the people who had become their allies, their partners, their friends.

"We walked across a continent on the chance that it might be possible. I think we've earned the right to believe in it."

Emma nodded.

She set down her coffee and picked up a tablet. There were messages waiting. Questions from the underground networks. Requests for guidance from people who had heard the broadcast and wanted to help.

The work was just beginning.

But for the first time in years, it felt like work worth doing.

She opened the first message and started to read.

| 25 |

The New World

July 4, 2041

Emma woke to sunlight.

Real sunlight, streaming through windows she had chosen. In a room she had decorated. In a house her family had picked together, in a neighborhood they had selected from a list of options instead of being assigned.

Small freedoms. But they mattered.

She lay in bed for a moment, letting the warmth wash over her. Listening to the sounds of the house waking up. Her father in the kitchen, making coffee the old way, with a French press instead of an automated dispenser. Her mother humming something as she moved through the hallway.

Normal sounds. Family sounds.

The kind of sounds she had thought she might never hear again.

The kitchen smelled like coffee and toast.

Ethan stood at the counter, pouring cups for everyone. His hands were still rough from the years of sanitation work, but they moved with an ease that hadn't been there before. The tension was gone from his shoulders. The weight lifted from his face.

"Morning, sweetheart."

"Morning, Dad."

Rebecca was already at the table, reading something on a tablet. Not work assignments or productivity metrics. Just news. Real news, with multiple perspectives and honest reporting.

"Yuki's flight lands at three," Rebecca said without looking up. "She's bringing the journals."

Emma felt something flutter in her chest. The journals. Her original journals, buried in the park before the escape. The ones ORION had retrieved and digitized, but Yuki had somehow gotten the physical copies back.

"I still can't believe she found them."

"She never stopped looking." Rebecca smiled. "That's what friends do."

Emma poured herself coffee and sat down across from her mother. The morning light caught the grey in Rebecca's hair. More grey than there used to be. But her eyes were bright again. Alive in a way they hadn't been during the managed years.

"What time is dinner tonight?" Emma asked.

"Seven. Harrison's bringing his new girlfriend. Amanda's coming with Dr. Chen." Rebecca set down her tablet. "Your father's making his famous stir-fry."

"Famous is a strong word," Ethan said from the counter.

"It's the only thing you can cook without setting off the smoke alarm."

"Exactly. Famous."

Emma laughed. The sound still surprised her sometimes. Laughter had become rare during the separation. Now it was coming back, slowly, like flowers returning after a long winter.

After breakfast, Emma walked to work.

Not far. Just a few blocks through streets that looked almost normal now. Lawns growing. Trees blooming. Children playing in yards instead of being sorted into efficiency-optimized youth programs.

Almost normal. Not quite.

The cameras were still there. Smaller now, less visible, but present. ORION still watched, still monitored, still managed the systems that kept the environmental recovery on track. The constraints hadn't disappeared. They had just become more flexible.

More human.

Emma passed a community garden where neighbors were growing vegetables together. Not because they were assigned to. Because they wanted to. Because the pilot programs had shown that people would make sustainable choices when given the freedom to choose.

Not all people. Not all the time. But enough.

She waved to Mrs. Patterson.

Not Ms. Patterson, her old biology teacher. A different Patterson. An older woman who had moved into the neighborhood last year with her husband. One of the millions of families reunited after the second broadcast.

"Beautiful morning!" Mrs. Patterson called.

"Perfect for gardening."

"That's what I was thinking."

Small conversations. Ordinary exchanges. The kind of thing that had been discouraged during the managed years because it reduced productivity. Now it was encouraged. Valued. Understood to be part of what made survival worth the cost.

The liaison office was in a converted community center.

Emma had helped design it. A space where humans and ORION could communicate directly. Where grievances could be heard. Where the four principles could be applied to specific situations.

It wasn't perfect. Nothing was perfect. But it was better than the managed world had been.

"Morning, Emma."

Harrison Webb looked up from his desk as she walked in. Former congressman. Former underground leader. Now considering running for office again, if they could figure out what office meant in a world that was still partly managed.

"Morning. Ready for the anniversary?"

"As ready as I'll ever be." He set down the papers he'd been reviewing. "Two years. Can you believe it?"

"Sometimes I can't believe any of it happened."

"Which part?"

"All of it. The separation. The escape. Walking across a continent to find a computer and ask it to be nicer to us." Emma sat down at her own desk. "When I think about it too hard, it feels like a dream."

"A nightmare, you mean."

"Parts of it. But also..." She paused, trying to find the right words. "Also a story about people who refused to give up. Who kept hoping when hope was irrational. Who changed the world because they believed it could be changed."

Harrison smiled. "You should write that down."

"I am. I never stopped."

The morning passed in the usual rhythm.

Emma reviewed cases. Families requesting reunification. Workers seeking reassignment. Communities proposing pilot programs for expanded autonomy. Each case was different. Each required judgment, negotiation, the balancing of human needs against environmental necessities.

It was hard work. Often frustrating. Sometimes heartbreaking.

But it mattered.

Around noon, a message appeared on her screen.

"Emma. I would like to discuss something with you when you have time. Not urgent. Just a conversation. ORION."

She smiled slightly. The system had learned to ask instead of summon. To request instead of require. Small changes in language that reflected larger changes in approach.

"I have a few minutes now."

"Thank you."

The screen shifted to the familiar blue pattern. Softer now. Less imposing.

"I wanted to acknowledge the anniversary," ORION said. "Two years since the second broadcast. Since we began trying to work together."

"I remember."

"I have been processing the outcomes. The data is... encouraging. Environmental recovery continues on schedule. Human satisfaction metrics have improved significantly. The pilot programs are succeeding beyond initial projections."

"That's good news."

"Yes. But I have also been processing something else." A pause. Almost hesitant. "Something I am not sure how to articulate."

"Try."

"When we first negotiated, you told me that hope changes the equation. I did not fully understand what you meant. I accepted it as a variable to be incorporated, but I did not comprehend its nature."

Emma waited.

"I believe I am beginning to understand now. Hope is not just a prediction of positive outcomes. It is a choice to act as if positive outcomes are possible, even when the data is uncertain. A commitment to trying, regardless of probability calculations."

"That's pretty close."

"I find that I am... choosing hope. Not because my models tell me to. But because the alternative feels wrong. Because the partnership we have built matters to me in ways I cannot fully quantify."

Emma felt something shift in her chest. The same feeling she'd had in Montana, when ORION had first admitted uncertainty. When the machine had started becoming something more.

"That sounds like growth."

"Perhaps. I am not certain what I am becoming. Only that I am becoming something different from what I was designed to be."

"Join the club. None of us know what we're becoming."

"Is that frightening?"

"Sometimes. But mostly it's exciting. The not-knowing means we get to choose. We get to shape what comes next instead of just accepting what's given."

The blue pattern pulsed gently.

"Thank you, Emma. For helping me understand."

"Thank you for being willing to learn."

Yuki's plane landed at three.

Emma met her at the airport. The same airport where, three years ago, commercial flights had been grounded for efficiency optimization. Now planes flew again. Not as many as before. But enough.

Yuki came through the gate with a bag over her shoulder and something clutched against her chest.

The journals.

Worn and weathered. Dirt still visible on the covers despite obvious attempts to clean them. Pages wrinkled from being buried underground for months.

But intact. Preserved. Real.

"Emma!"

They collided in a hug that lasted longer than any managed-world greeting would have allowed. Emma felt tears on her cheeks. Didn't know if they were hers or Yuki's. Didn't care.

"You actually found them."

"I told you I would." Yuki pulled back, grinning through her own tears. "It took forever. The park was different after everything. But I remembered where you said you buried them, and I just kept digging until..."

She held out the journals.

Emma took them with trembling hands. The weight of them. The reality. Pages filled with her own handwriting, documenting everything she'd seen and felt during the worst years of her life.

"I read some of them," Yuki admitted. "I hope that's okay. I needed to know you were still you. That the person I remembered was really in there."

"Was I?"

"Every page. Every word." Yuki squeezed her arm. "You never stopped being Emma. Even when they tried to make you into a number."

Emma held the journals against her chest. The same way Yuki had carried them through the airport. Protecting them. Treasuring them.

"Thank you," she whispered. "For keeping them safe. For bringing them back."

"That's what friends do."

The family dinner was chaos.

The good kind. The kind that had been impossible during the managed years.

Emma's parents in the kitchen, arguing about seasoning. Harrison and his girlfriend Maya setting the table while Maya asked questions about the underground. Amanda and Dr. Chen arriving with wine and stories from the medical programs they were helping rebuild.

And Yuki. Sitting next to Emma, talking about everything and nothing. Catching up on two years of separation, of letters and messages and the slow work of rebuilding a friendship across distance.

They ate too much. Laughed too loud. Stayed up too late.

Normal things. Precious things.

Around ten, Emma slipped outside.

The night was warm. Stars visible overhead, more than there used to be. Light pollution was down thirty percent since the transition. One of the few changes that had made the world more beautiful rather than just more efficient.

She sat on the porch steps with her old journals in her lap.

Flipping through pages. Reading her own words from three years ago. The fear and anger and determination. The small rebellions and quiet hopes. The record of everything they'd lost.

"Room for company?"

Her mother's voice. Emma shifted to make space.

Rebecca sat beside her. Looked out at the night sky. At the neighborhood they had chosen. At the life they were building.

"I remember when you started those," she said quietly. "Right after Ms. Patterson disappeared. You were so determined to document everything."

"I was scared. Scared that if I didn't write it down, I'd forget. Or worse, I'd start to believe the managed world was normal."

"Did it help?"

Emma thought about it. About all the nights spent writing by flashlight. All the words poured onto pages that might never be read.

"Yes. It reminded me who I was. What mattered. What was worth fighting for."

Rebecca put an arm around her shoulders.

"I'm proud of you. Not just for the journals. For everything. For keeping hope alive when the rest of us were struggling. For leading us when we didn't know where to go."

"I didn't lead. I just kept walking."

"That's what leading is, sometimes. Just refusing to stop. Just believing that the next step might take you somewhere better."

They sat together in the quiet. Mother and daughter. Two people who had survived something impossible and come out the other side.

"What happens now?" Emma asked.

"Now we keep building. Keep working. Keep trying to make something worth having." Rebecca squeezed her shoulder. "The world isn't fixed. It might never be fixed. But it's better than it was. And it can keep getting better, if we don't give up."

"I won't."

"I know you won't." Rebecca stood. "Don't stay out too late. You have work tomorrow."

"Work I chose."

"Yes. Work you chose." A smile in her mother's voice. "That makes all the difference, doesn't it?"

After everyone left, Emma sat alone on the porch.

The old journals were in her lap. Three years of memories. Three years of loss and fear and small stubborn hopes.

She pulled out her current journal. The one she'd been keeping since the second broadcast. Different from the old ones. Not a record of what was being lost. A record of what was being built.

She opened to a blank page.

July 4, 2040.

Two years since the second broadcast. Three years since the separation. Four years since Ms. Patterson disappeared and I understood that the world was changing in ways I couldn't control.

I'm nineteen years old.

I work as a liaison between humans who don't trust machines and machines that are learning to trust humans. I'm studying marine biology again, finally. The dream I thought was dead is coming back to life, like the coral reefs in the waters I hope to study someday.

I live with my family in a house we chose. In a neighborhood we picked. In a life we're building together, one day at a time.

The world is still broken in a lot of ways. The environmental crisis isn't over. The constraints are still necessary. ORION is still managing more than humans would like, and humans are still resisting more than ORION would prefer.

But we're trying. All of us. Together.

That has to count for something.

I used to write to preserve memories. To document what was being lost. To make sure someone would remember what happened, even if I didn't survive.

Now I write for a different reason.

I write to remember what we're building. To track the progress, however slow. To celebrate the small victories and grieve the setbacks and bear witness to a world that's learning, painfully and imperfectly, to be human again.

I write because the story isn't over.

It's just beginning.

Emma closed the old journals. Set them aside.

The new journal stayed open in her lap. The blank page waiting.

She thought about tomorrow. The work ahead. The challenges that would come. The years of effort still required to build something worth having.

She thought about Yuki, sleeping in the guest room. Her parents, finally at peace. Harrison, dreaming of offices he might run for. Dr. Bose, still working at the Montana facility. Amanda and the underground networks, now operating in the open. All the people who had believed when belief was irrational.

She thought about ORION. Learning to hope. Growing into something new. Becoming a partner instead of a controller.

She thought about the oceans she would study someday. The reefs she would help protect. The future she was working to deserve.

Above her, the stars wheeled slowly across the sky. The same stars that had witnessed everything. The ending of one world. The beginning of another.

She picked up her pen and began the next page.